HARTLEY

P9-AOY-911

THE BIRTH OF A LEGEND...

They were cantering along in the snow, as Butch tried out possibilities for Longabaugh's new name. "Cherokee Charlie . . . Buck Barton . . . Johnny Ringo." He shook his head. "Already taken. Lucky Wilson . . ."

Now Longabaugh shook his head.

Butch continued, annoyed. "Well, then, will you help? I need a little inspiration here. Haven't you ever done anything interesting?"

"I was in jail once."

"Where?"

"Sundance, Wyoming."

"Kid Sundance," Butch said. Then, "The Sundance Kid." The two men looked at each other.

"I like that," Longabaugh said.

"So do I," Butch replied. "In fact, I like it so much *I* want it. You can be Butch Cassidy."

"Nope, it's mine," Longabaugh insisted stubbornly. "I was in jail there, not you, so I get it." His smile dazzled as he pushed his hat jauntily forward. "The Sundance Kid," he said proudly. "The Sundance Kid."

BUTCH AND SUNDANCE
THE EARLY DAYS

A Novel
by
D. R. Bensen

Based on a Screenplay
by
Allan Burns

A DELL BOOK

XXX
North York Public Library
Don Mills   SEP 8 0

Published by
Dell Publishing Co., Inc.
1 Dag Hammarskjold Plaza
New York, New York 10017

Copyright © 1979 by William Goldman

All rights reserved. No part of this book may be reproduced or
transmitted in any form or by any means, electronic or mechanical,
including photocopying, recording or by any information storage
and retrieval system, without the written permission of the
Publisher, except where permitted by law.

Dell ® TM 681510, Dell Publishing Co., Inc.

ISBN: 0-440-10865-9

Printed in Canada

First printing—May 1979

BUTCH AND SUNDANCE
THE EARLY DAYS

CHAPTER ONE

A prison is never quiet. Even at night, the sounds of forty or so men sleeping, or trying to sleep, in one enclosed space—two to a cell, ten cells on each side of a stone-paved corridor—carry remarkably. The cougher in Cell 2 can be heard as clearly in Cell 20 as by his bunkmate; a groan and rattling rustle caused by the man in Cell 7 trying to find a position in which the straw in his mattress does not poke into his shoulder blade is shared by all. It is probably something about the acoustics: stone walls, ceilings and floors, and steel bars reflect and transmit sound enthusiastically but without much precision. Rugs on the floors and drapes or hangings on the walls would absorb much of the sound, but few prison administrators, if any, seem to feel that this touch of gracious living is worthwhile. Certainly the warden of the Wyoming State Penitentiary in this year of 1896 did not.

Most of the prisoners would not have minded the normal run of nighttime noises; almost all had been cowboys, and would be again once their terms were up, and were used to being packed in bunkhouses with a dozen or more uneasy sleepers. But the top-bunk occupant of Cell 13 was adding a new and dreadful element to the chorus.

"They's fourteen verses to that song," 18 (lower bunk) muttered to his cellmate, "and I b'lieve he's goin' t' play every one of 'em."

"It could be the same one over an' over again," Up-

7

per said. "Without the words, you got no way of knowin' whether he's at the part about walkin' out in the streets of Laredo or gettin' six cowpunchers to carry him along."

"How you expect him to sing whiles as he's playin' a mouth organ?" Lower asked. "He's some smart, I guess, but I don't see him carryin' that one off, no, sir. Words an' tune'd just sort of bubble out in a godalmighty mess."

The harmonicist blew a note that had no relationship to any that had gone before or would follow.

"Worse'n *that?*" Upper said.

"Will you shut *up!*" a man at the other end of the corridor yelled.

"You been playin' that thing for a *year,* Parker, an' you *never* git any better!" another critic called.

"I'll play a little softer," a voice answered mildly. "Lemme know if this bothers you."

The off-key rendition of the Cowboy's Lament resumed, then broke off with a heavy thump, a sliding noise, and another thump. The prisoners' practiced ears accurately interpreted this sequence of sounds as evidence that the musician's cellmate, maddened beyond endurance, had booted the bunk above him, tipping man and mattress onto the floor.

"A simple yes or no would of been enough," a plaintive voice said.

"Funny about music," Upper 18 said. "If it ain't just *so,* it'll drive you crazy. But when it's done right, it'll make you feel good like nothin' else. Charms to soothe the savage beast, like they say."

"That's 'breast,' ain't it?" Lower asked.

"What is?"

"Soothe the savage *breast,* not *beast.*"

"It don't do to talk about such things in here," Upper said severely, and, in the comparative silence, wrapped his blanket closer and composed himself for sleep.

In Cell 13, the harmonicist, back in his bunk, stared up into the darkness. By God, if everything went right in the morning, he'd be playing the old mouth organ in the open air tomorrow—and a sight more cheerful tune, too! He wondered if he still remembered the tricky tonguing for *Oh, Susannah!* . . .

"What's the Governor want with you?" the guard walking next to him asked, unlocking a heavy steel door, escorting him through, then clanging it shut.

"My counsel an' advice on how to deal with the plague of bad men that is givin' Wyoming a unsavory reputation," the prisoner said. "Come all the way on the cars from Cheyenne to get the benefit of my wisdom an' experience."

"It's his reg'lar day to look in here," the guard said. "An' I don't see old Richards is goin' to learn much from a man that's drawed a deuce for horse stealin'—*that* don't count for much in the way of experience." He unlocked another steel door, passed himself and his prisoner through it, and relocked it. They were now in the administrative section of the prison. It was a year since the prisoner had walked on wooden floors or seen pictures hung on walls, and he gave an interested glance at the framed steel engravings of views of Laramie and its ornament, the penitentiary. It looked a lot better seen from the outside than from within.

"Horse stealing was all they *proved* against me," he said. "Governor Richards is long-headed enough to know that a man's reputation counts for something, too."

"What kind of advice could *you* give him?" the guard said, unsure whether to take the comment seriously. That broad, cheerful young face always radiated sincerity, even when a man *knew* it was emitting pure sheep-dip.

"For one, how to get rid of one hardcase, permanent."

"They done that last week, with Wind River Slim," the guard said. "Walked him up thirteen steps and down one, then planted him, permanent as you please."

"I'm not about to suggest anything so crude as hanging," the prisoner said, offended. "Seeing as it's me I got in mind."

The guard glared at him, then rapped on the paneled golden-oak door in front of which they had halted. He waited a few seconds, then opened it, pushed the prisoner through, and said, "Parker, Governor."

He closed the door and stood against it.

The prisoner nodded amiably to the solidly built, elegantly dressed man who sat behind the warden's desk, and to the warden himself, seated in a chair to one side. For good measure he gave a third nod, to a convict who was perched on a trellis outside the window behind the Governor, cleaning the panes industriously—the same pane over and over again, in fact—as he goggled at the proceedings in the office.

The Governor finally looked up and said in an unemotional tone, "Robert LeRoy Parker."

The prisoner nodded once more.

"Alias Butch Cassidy."

Another nod, this time accompanied by a broad smile.

"Where'd you pick up a name like Butch?" the Governor asked.

"I worked in a butcher shop when I was goin' straight once, so, you see, they called me—"

"Well, yes." The Governor stared at him intently. Butch shifted his weight from foot to foot, and made an effort not to look away.

"You want me to parole you."

"Yessir, I do," Butch said earnestly.

"Well, I *could* do that," the Governor said. "Or you could stay in here and serve out the rest of your sentence." He glanced down at the papers before him on the desk and looked up. "Another year."

Butch nodded shortly. It seemed to him that Richards had covered all trails on that one: go or stay, that was what it came down to. If the Governor had just now worked that out, he must not be what you would call a lightning calculator; but maybe politicians always liked to say something obvious when they started talking, so you wouldn't notice if they got tricky later on.

"This is the only time you've been in prison," the Governor went on. "For horse theft, it says."

Butch nodded again. Now that the Governor had it clear that *he* was doing time, *why*, and for how *long*, and that he wanted to get *out*, they were in a position to get on with the business of the day.

"Even though," the Governor added drily, "you're suspected of three train holdups and six bank robberies."

"Six? *Twelve*'s more like it."

The prisoner turned quickly to face the source of the new voice; the guard at the door tensed, then relaxed as the prisoner grinned and waved at the gaunt man in work clothes with a star pinned to his vest who sat in a dim, far corner of the room, holding his broad-brimmed hat in his lap.

The Governor said, still consulting the Cassidy file, "Sheriff Bledsoe here—I believe you know each other—"

"Yessir," Butch said enthusiastically. "He's the one that arrested me. Hi, Ray, good to see you."

" 'Lo, Butch," Bledsoe said quietly.

"Thought you were working out of Utah now," Butch said with interest.

"I am."

The Governor coughed, and Cassidy turned to face him. "Sheriff Bledsoe," Richards said, "rode all the way up here when he heard you were up for parole."

11

"Hey," Butch said, giving Bledsoe a pleased look. "How about that?"

"He told me something interesting," Richards went on. "He says he let you out of jail the night before you were brought here. That right?"

"Yessir."

Richards frowned toward the corner. "Why'd you do that, Sheriff?"

Bledsoe crumpled and uncrumpled the brim of his hat. "He asked me to."

"So you did?" Richards asked. "Just like that?"

The sheriff nodded.

"Weren't you afraid he'd use that time to try and get away?"

"No," Bledsoe said.

Butch grinned. Whether he was talking to a fellow he'd just parted the hair of with a bullet before arresting him—Butch could still feel the scar along his scalp—or to the Governor of one of the forty-four states, Ray wasn't *about* to waste any words. Hadn't even bothered to say "Come on" to Butch that night over near Lander, while Butch was lying on the ground, trying to figure if his brains were leaking out the top of his head—just made a get-up-and-over-there gesture with the still-warm barrel of his Winchester.

"Why not?" said the Governor.

"Because I promised him I wouldn't," Butch cut in. No sense obliging Ray to make a whole long speech like that if he didn't have to.

Governor Richards, after a quick, cold glance at Butch, turned back to Bledsoe. "And you believed him?"

"Yessir." Bledsoe paused, then resigned himself to the need for talkativeness. "I've always known Butch to be an honorable fellow." Sensing, from the Governor's hard stare, that this comment had not gone down well, he added, "For a horse thief."

The Governor drummed his fingers on the table,

and looked hard at the prisoner and then at Bledsoe. The convict window cleaner, Butch saw, now had the top sash open a crack, and was enthralled by the high drama being enacted in front of him.

Governor Richards gazed ruminatively at the desktop, then at the still-silent warden, who was doing his best to look as if nothing that had taken place in his office in the last five minutes had anything to do with him.

After a long moment, he looked back to Butch. "You promise to stay on the right side of the law," he said slowly, "and I'll parole you right now. Tell me you'll go straight and you'll be free this morning."

Butch took a deep breath and said, "I can't do that."

Watching the Governor's face go tight and his eyes widen, Butch was also aware that Bledsoe had jumped up from his chair.

"What!" the sheriff said.

"Why not?" asked Richards.

The convict at the window dropped his sponge, then resumed his work, employing the tail of his shirt.

"I wouldn't mean it," Butch explained earnestly. He turned to Bledsoe. "Ray, you *know* I tried going straight once, but I couldn't do it. I mean, that butcher shop, it just wasn't what I'm cut out to do."

Bledsoe, his large hands twisting his hat into something that resembled a dried cowpat more than it did a lawman's headgear, spoke agitatedly. "Now, look here, Butch, the Governor *wants* to let you out of here, but you got to meet him halfway!"

Butch shook his head slowly, and faced Richards once more. "I know, but it'd be a *lie*, sir." His face shone with the virtue of the young George Washington explaining that untruth was foreign to him. "But listen," he said, "I'll tell you what I *can* do."

The Governor's eyebrows shortened the distance between themselves and his hairline by half.

"I'll make you a deal—"

"Butch!" Bledsoe said warningly. "This is the *Governor* . . ."

Butch's right hand accorded this interruption a quick wave that said "*I* know that" as clearly as if the words had been spoken.

"No, listen," he went on, his eyes aglow with earnestness. "I promise you . . . if you let me out, I'll never break the law in *your* state again! Isn't that what you want?"

"Well, uh, yes," the Governor said faintly. Looked at one way, it made sense. The public well-being in Wyoming was his responsibility, and if his constituency could be preserved from this fast-talking young daredevil at the price of a year's remission from his sentence, it might not be a bad trade, especially in an election year. On the other hand, turning loose a man determined to pursue the owlhoot trail amounted to giving him a license to prey on all the country's remaining states, territories and possessions, including Alaska and the Midway Islands. . . . "But there are—" he began.

"I swear to God I'll leave this state *alone*," Butch said. "*Promise.*" He held his right hand shoulder-high for a second, his spread-out left seeming to search for a Bible to validate his commitment. "Even if the *mint* train was to come through Wyoming, I wouldn't touch it." He looked toward Bledsoe. "Would I, now, Ray?"

The Governor was looking hard at Bledsoe. So also were the convict perched outside the window and the guard at the door. The warden, who had not moved or spoken during the unusual interview, continued to regard the wall opposite him with a notable lack of interest. If governors and sheriffs and prisoners chose to use his office as a forum for debate and the making of irregular and perhaps unlawful deals, his posture seemed to state eloquently, it was none of *his* business.

Bledsoe took a deep breath and said slowly, "I'd tend to believe him."

"See?" Butch said triumphantly.

"I just . . ." the Governor said.

"On my *honor*."

Richards looked once more toward the sheriff. "But . . . I mean . . . well . . ."

Bledsoe shrugged, then gave a slow nod.

"Come *on*," Butch wheedled. He leaned toward the Governor, displaying the righteous confidence of a lad who *knows* that he deserves the Scripture-recitation prize in Sunday School. The Governor studied his face, then Bledsoe's expectant countenance—and then, his eye caught by a flicker of shadow on the wall in front of him, he turned and glared at the openly eavesdropping window cleaner. The convict looked quickly away, then back, as if he had just noticed the room and its occupants, and bent to dab at the bottom panes of the window with his shirttail, giving the Governor only the top of his head to singe with his gaze.

Richards gave the silent warden a glance of disfavor and muttered, "I don't see that being in this place a year longer would do much of anything for you, Parker, or for the State of Wyoming. If we can get shut of you for good and all by turning you loose, I suppose it's as good a bargain as we can expect."

"*Thank* you, Governor," Butch said, smiling broadly. "I'll tell you straight, you won't regret it, no, *sir*."

The Governor nodded glumly. Cassidy, or Parker, was very likely right, he felt. The Governors of Utah, Colorado, Idaho, New Mexico, and Arizona, though, probably wouldn't thank him if they knew what he'd done. But that was their lookout. . . .

CHAPTER TWO

Butch slowed the horse to a trot and turned to look behind him. The homestead he had passed a while back was out of sight now, sunk below the flat horizon of the plains—nothing but grass and sage and the prairie wild flowers there now. And ahead of him, patches of white along the summit blazing in the early-afternoon sun, lay the Medicine Bow range.

"Nothing and no*body*," he said aloud, delightedly. A whole year of walls and bars and breathing in air dozens of other men had used before . . . and it was over. Out here, there was just Butch Cassidy and the open sky, and not so much as a telegraph wire to show that he wasn't the first man ever to pass this way.

He fished in his saddlebag for the harmonica. About the only thing he'd fetched away from the pen, not that he'd gone in with much. It was damned good of Ray, he reflected, to have brought his gear along to Laramie, and the money he'd had on him when he was taken. Without that—no great sum, all the same— he'd have had only the State's ten dollars, which was no stake at all for a young fellow with plans. This way, he'd had enough to buy this horse, stand Ray a good lunch and a couple of drinks, provision himself for a few days' riding, and see him through until those plans could bear some fruit.

Into the Medicine Bows about to Foxpark, then paralleling the U.P. tracks down to Colorado, maybe down as far as Hebron, then a couple of days' scramble

16

across the Divide into Steamboat Springs—that was the ticket. The Springs was the place to get word of what Elza and O.C. and the others might be up to—anything that was going on in the *buscadero* line.

Damn if he'd fiddle around widelooping horses and cows anymore, though. Rustling paid about five, six times what cowpunching did, average it out, only it entailed a number of dismaying hazards, such as the chance of being strung up from the nearest tree limb heavy enough for the job, or being dealt with even more unpleasantly if there weren't any trees handy. Risks were all right, Butch felt, but the thing was, they ought to be incurred in pursuit of something worthwhile. He had worked it out in prison: if money's what you're after, steal money, not animals.

He had the harmonica out now, and set it to his lips.

> *It rained all night the day I left,*
> *The weather, it was dry . . .*

He frowned and stopped playing. Back in jail, the old mouth organ had sounded okay, at least to him, never mind what the other jailbirds said. Maybe it had been the echoes or something, but the fact was that, out here in the open, it wasn't what you could call high-class music. He had taught himself the harmonica, to have something to do in the pen, and had been proud of learning to play by ear.

"Would of been better off learning to play by *mouth*," he muttered. He looked at the instrument, then shoved it into his pocket. He didn't need it for consolation now, and it wasn't much fun doing something badly.

"Do what you're good at, an' stay away from what you *ain't* good at," he reasoned aloud, "an' that's the way to get on in this world, Mister Cassidy. An' by God and by glory, ain't I just on my *way!*"

He gave an exultant whoop, dug his heels into the horse's flanks, and set it pounding toward the mountains ahead.

An hour later, the sun still above the nearby peaks, he slid from the saddle by the bank of a mountain stream. A waterfall cascading down a twenty-foot drop had scoured out a pool in the stream bed.

"Hoo!" he said, sliding from the saddle. "Don't know's I ever rode so fast without a posse being after me!" Well, there had been a year of prison to sweat out of him, and the hard riding was just the thing to do it. He wiped his damp forehead with his sleeve and tossed his hat, soaked with sweat, onto the ground.

He led the horse downstream to where it could reach the surface of the water and left it gulping thirstily. Then he climbed back to the ledge above the pool and stripped off his boots and sweaty clothing, retaining only the knee-length drawers. "Get me a bath an' a little laundering at one an' the same time," he said happily.

He stood a moment at the pool's edge, letting the cool mountain air wash over him, savoring the warmth of the sun on his back. The thunder of the waterfall and the fine tingle of its spray on his skin were compelling, intoxicating; the surface of the pool rippled below him, inviting him to cleanse himself of everything left of the past year.

He crouched, brought his arms forward and up, and dove, splitting the surface cleanly.

"Eeehaah!"

He came half out of the water, leaping like a harpooned whale, flailed himself to the nearest bank in a flurry of foam, and clawed his way up.

That's the thing about prison, Cassidy, he told himself angrily. Turns your brains to *mush*. Me that's known this country twenty-some years, man and boy, and forgetting what happens when you jump into a

18

stream that's coming straight down from the snow-fields!

Mumbling imprecations, he picked his way across the rocky ground, wincing as the sharp-edged pebbles cut into the soles of his feet. "Damn jail turns a man back into a tenderfoot, too. . . ." He reached the heap of clothes he had flung down, picked up his pants, and began to blot himself dry. He pulled off the soaking drawers, wrung them out, and spread them on a flat rock that caught the sunlight, then sat down in the same patch of sun.

In a few moments, his irritable mood passed. Even if that stream could freeze a man solid in nothing flat, it surely looked and sounded pretty; and the air, sliding around him like a slower-moving, thinner form of water, carried a sharp, clean, resinous scent. He took a deep breath, let it out, and felt himself beginning to relax—really relax, the way he hadn't since before Ray Bledsoe's bullet had creased him and he'd been turned into Convict No. 187.

"Got somethin' to think about," he mused aloud. "Jumping into the water like that without takin' mind of what I *knew* it'd be like, that was a fool stunt. I *looked* before I leaped, all right, just like they say you should. Trouble was, I wasn't *seeing* what I was looking at. Now that's no way for a man's brains to be working if he's figuring to get on the robbing trade, for sure. You got to *plan*, Cassidy. Think out all the moves . . . an' then a move ahead."

He brooded until a sudden chill told him that the sun had passed behind the peaks to the west, then hurriedly dressed and began preparing his camp for the night.

The sun was almost directly overhead, and struck fiery glints from the steel rails twelve feet below where he lay prone on the narrow rock ledge; but the pines that pressed almost to the edge of the gorge whose walls rose above him shaded him. His horse whickered from where it was tied to a tree near the rim. When the sound faded, he heard the noise he had been waiting for: the click-clack of the rails as they transmitted the news of an approaching train. On time: departs Albany 11:50, arrives Foxpark 12:36. Cassidy grinned; it had taken some doing to get that fistful of railroad schedules back in Laramie without Ray Bledsoe noticing and maybe asking awkward questions about what use he planned to make of them.

He squirmed toward the edge of the ledge, keeping flat. He could hear the chuffing of the engine as it pulled the train upgrade through the twisting gorge.

Now it came in sight around the nearest bend, fat truncated-diamond stack belching smoke and sparks. He was above the line of sight of the engineer, whose long-billed cap he could see as the man leaned out of the cab to check the track ahead. He'd picked a good spot, all right. A jump from here would set him down neatly on the locomotive's rear platform as it passed, going no more than ten miles an hour on the grade. With two six-guns covering them, the engineer and fireman wouldn't give any trouble—at the next handy spot, they'd stop the train as ordered, while the others dealt with the baggage car and whatever might be in its safe. No sense in taking up a collection among the passengers—that tripled the risks of having to shoot somebody, especially if there were women there and some fellow got the notion it wasn't manly to be buffaloed in front of a lady, and it didn't increase the takings that much.

A cloud of smoke and cinders blew across the ledge and stung his eyes; then the stack was moving right by him, and the sleek length of the boiler. Now the cab roof was beneath him; then he was looking down on the sweat-stained back of the fireman, heaving coal from the tender into the firebox—right *there* was the spot to jump to . . .

He relaxed, grimaced, and shied a pebble at the roof of the baggage car.

Oh, it was a *great* setup for a train robbery, all right, neat and workmanlike, nobody hurt, and no hard feelings except from the Union Pacific and the express company, which most folks would as soon see get a bloody nose now and then anyhow.

If, that is, a man happened to have a six-gun or so on him, and a couple of partners to side him. The way things were, he was like a kid pressing his nose against the candy-store window, and no penny in his pocket.

"Well, hell," he said aloud. "I promised the Governor I wouldn't do anything contumacious and unlawful in his state, an' so I ain't. But it's not much fun keeping your word when you got no choice about it!"

The last car was out of sight now, and he rose, stretched, and began the climb up the wall of the gorge to where his horse was tethered.

A couple of days and he'd be in Steamboat Springs—well into Colorado, where his undertaking to Governor Richards didn't hold. Some hard going across the Divide, but worth it. At the Springs, he'd be able to equip himself suitably, get word of current business opportunities, and set about recruiting the sort of staff those opportunities called for. One real partner—a fellow who'd have the kind of drive and nerve, the killer instinct, if it came to that, that would fit in with Butch's own talent for planning and his quirky way of looking at things—that was the key to what he wanted to do. A solid sidekick with him, and nothing would be beyond reach! And Steamboat Springs was the place to start looking. . . .

Well, it depends what you're looking for," the clerk said. "We got considerable call for this number." He displayed a single-shot derringer which fit neatly in the palm of his hand. "A man needs a convincing answer in a sudden dispute that comes up 'twixt him and

21

an acquaintance, as it might be at the card table, and this little buster can come sliding out of your sleeve or your boot top, even from under your hat, slick as you please, and you got at the worst a Mex standoff. Should you be carrying a brace of 'em, you can make your point with one feller and still have a pretty strong argument left for any survivors."

"I don't know as I propose to get involved in card-playing and socializing all that serious," Butch told him. "A plain old six-shooter'll suit me fine."

"You can't do better than this," the gunsmith's clerk said, bringing out a weapon, its blued steel agleam like some precious gem from front sight to butt plate, and hefting it with a connoisseur's appreciation. "Colt's Frontiersman, very popular model, renowned for accuracy and ease of handlin'. Costs you some, but it's worth it. You get what you pay for, it's a law of nature, not to mention business."

"I was thinking of something a little more . . ."

The clerk sighed, returned the handsome revolver to its shelf, and brought out a considerably dingier, cruder-looking pistol. "Unless you're goin' to drop into the popgun class, this is the cheapest we got. It'll work, and shoot reasonable straight, and that's about as much as you can say for it."

"Fills the bill for me," Butch said cheerfully, counting out with care the price the clerk named. "How about some loads for it?"

The clerk set a box of cartridges on the counter and slid it to him. "That'll be . . ." He stopped, his lips tightening, as Butch opened the box and counted out six cartridges and placed them in the pistol's cylinder, then selected another half-dozen and stuck them in the cartridge loops of his worn gunbelt.

"Supposing I was to get unlucky," he said, pushing the partly emptied box back to the clerk, "then it'd of been a waste to of made a heavy investment of working capital in something I wasn't goin' to use, now wouldn't it?"

Outside, he stepped along the plankwalk, enjoying the solid weight of the gun at his waist. Some persnickety of old Ray not to let him pick one up in Laramie, where he could have made a better deal, most likely, but the sheriff had been firm. "You promised the Governor you wouldn't break the law in Wyoming again," he said, "and I know you *mean* to keep your word. But you don't want to take a chance on sufferin' a sudden loss of memory and happenin' to find yourself with a gun in your hand and some feller handin' over his valuables, do you, Butch?" And he had stayed with Butch every moment until Butch had ridden out of town.

Even though the sun was high, the air was cool, and Butch shivered at the memory of the last few nights. It had been *cold* coming through the mountains, and blankets he'd wrapped around himself at night had just about kept him from freezing solid, but not much more. Still some more outfitting to do . . .

He turned off the plankwalk at Diggs' Emporium— Dry Goods, Sundries & Feed—and bought a thigh-length sheepskin jacket. Afoot or in the saddle, a man could hunch down in it and turn up the collar, and be warm and dry, no matter what the weather. Paying for it shrank his roll of bills noticeably, and he sighed. No time at all before he'd have to start in putting those plans of his into action and get down to work. Going straight or otherwise, there was no getting out of it: work, or don't eat.

He stopped at the candy counter and bought a handful of raisins, declining the salesgirl's offer to put them in a paper sack—that'd be a sight, Butch Cassidy ambling down the main street of Steamboat Springs with a bag of sweets in his hand! With every other man in town a rustler or some kind of hardcase, he'd wind up being called the Candy Kid or some such. He opened the jacket's side pocket and motioned the sales-girl to dump the raisins in it. He couldn't understand her look of distaste—the jacket was new, after all. Of course, after he'd had it a while, it was true enough that you'd be leery of dropping anything you meant to eat in the pockets; it was a wonder, the kind of stuff that seemed practically to *grow* in the bottom of a pocket.

Out in the sun again, he munched a raisin. Little bit of a lamb-chop taste to it, but not bad.

Butch poked his head in above the batwings of the nearest saloon, identified by its sign simply as Anderson's. Looked like the right kind of place, but nobody there now except a couple of storekeepers taking a late-morning refresher and an untidy bundle of rags at the far end of the bar. Like a desert flower between rains, it would remain in that state until somebody stuck a drink in front of it; then it would pull itself together and sit up and be revealed as something nearly human, ready to pay for its refreshment with a rambling yarn about the big gold strike it had once made, only to be swindled by Eastern trusts or a faith-less partner.

Butch withdrew his head and gave an inward shud-der. There weren't all that many greenbacks between him and that bum right now. . . . After dark, that would be the time to drop in here, size the crowd up, and start in on the next step.

Meanwhile, there were some hours to kill. What did a gentleman of leisure do with his time on an late-summer Steamboat Springs morning? From the sam-ples he saw, it seemed to amount to settling onto a comfortable bench, fence rail, or upturned barrel, se-lecting a choice straw, and chewing on it while survey-ing what there was of the passing scene.

Not much appeal in that, for sure. Butch had had, he felt, about ten years' worth of sitting still in the twelve months in the Laramie pen, and even the wearing journey through the Medicine Bows and across the Divide hadn't worn him out that much. He set off down the street, looking with interest at the shops and saloons, and enjoying the unaccustomed gesture of raising his hat when he passed a woman.

He soon found himself at the outskirts of town, where a few cleared but empty lots, one with a pile of lumber on it, showed that Steamboat Springs had plans for growing. On one lot was a wagon with a horse standing patiently in the shafts. One side of it was raised to form a roof, supported by poles; the exposed interior displayed a jumble of mysterious equipment and a worktable with a sink. The other side of the wagon bore in ornate lettering the legend: A. GRISSOM—PHOTOGRAPHY.

A whiskery, bald-headed man, presumably Grissom, sat perched on a stool in the shade of the raised wagon side; next to him was a large box, draped in black cloth, supported by a tripod. Butch was struck by the sight of a pile of paintings, about his height, that leaned against the wagon; the uppermost one showed a spindly sort of metal construction rising out of a queer-looking city, all stone buildings and wide streets.

"What's that s'posed to be?" he asked the photographer, jerking his thumb at the painting.

"Eiffel Tower, in Paris, France," Grissom said. "Very popular backdrop for them that'd like to have a photo showin' 'em off as world travelers."

"It's an eyeful, all right," Butch agreed. "What else you got?"

Grissom rose and flipped through the stretched canvases. "True-to-life rendition of the lounge and lobby of New York's famed Waldorf-Astoria Hotel . . . moonlight on the palms and beach at Pearl Harbor, Sandwich Islands . . . for customers that's got a taste that way, very realistic portrait of Lily Langtry in negligee, posed so as to be givin' the subject the glad eye. Accourse," he added, with a gesture toward the spectacular vista of mountains behind him, "you got a pretty good background right here, too."

"You could take a picture of me'd make me look like I was right over there in Paris, France?" Butch said. Now, that would be something—a picture like that would be a good reminder to a man that hard work and sound planning could make all kinds of dreams come true, just the way it used to say in *McGuffey's Eclectic Reader* in school.

"For a dollar and a half, I could," Grissom said.

"Well, now." Butch fished in his pocket and took out what coins he found there. They were a little sticky from the raisins, but it was easy enough to count them. "What I got here's about a dime short of a dollar. Can we dicker it down to that? 'S all I got." No lie, he told himself; it's all I got for frippery like this. It'd be downright immoral to dig into my working money.

Grissom glowered and shook his head.

"Lemme just stand in front of that tower painting a second," Butch said. "You take a look at me through that box thing, an' see what a swell picture I make, you'd be glad to cut your price. Make a second copy and you could use it to advertise with."

"No sense to it," Grissom grumbled. "But what the hell—no business today anyhow. Go stand there, and I'll tell you how the picture *would* of looked if you'd had the ready cash to pay for it."

Butch arranged himself in front of the Parisian backdrop. Grissom flipped the camera's black drape over his head and crouched behind it.

"How's this pose?" Butch called, drawing his revolver and aiming it squarely at the camera.

"It's—*oh*." Grissom's hands emerged from under the drape and rose straight in the air.

"Ninety-one cents strike you as a fair price, considering everything?" Butch asked.

"For an enterprisin' young feller like you," Grissom said in muffled but bitter tones, lowering his hands and withdrawing them under the drape, "I guess I can arrange a discount. Now hold *still*. I surely can't afford to waste a plate on *this* job."

Light, music, talk and laughter, the clink of glasses, and a glorious aroma of beer and spirits flooded out of Anderson's. Butch, on the point of entering, paused an instant and inhaled delightedly, then pushed his way in.

From the ceiling, almost two stories high, crystal-hung kerosene chandeliers blazed. About ten feet down, a balcony opening onto a corridor ran along one wall. Below it a five-piece orchestra, each performer tailcoated and white-tied, contended with the general din in a rendition of "Good-bye, Little Yellow Bird."

Butch threaded his way through the crowd to the long, ornately carved bar that extended almost the full length of one wall, and with a grin and a couple of deft hitches of his body managed to ease himself into a place against it without wounding the sensibilities of any of those already bellying up, and signed to the bartender that he'd have a shot of what the man next to him was enjoying.

When the drink came, he half-swallowed, half-inhaled it. Sipping whiskey, the like of which he hadn't experienced since early '95. All that the Laramie penitentiary had afforded in the way of spirituous dissipation was a batch of some popskull No. 208 Oblomov (aggravated assault, blasphemy, and something nobody wanted to talk about, to do with a mule: four years) had brewed out of potato peelings; Oblomov had said that the name for it in his folks' palaver was "little water," but, while it had looked like water, a couple of snorts produced the same result as having an axe helve swung against your head. All the same, in the Laramie pen, that put you ahead of the game.

He looked around the room, barnlike in its proportions, but obviously designed to gladden the hearts of pleasure-bent gentlemen rather than provide accommodations for the beasts of the field. In contrast to the elegantly decorated bar, the formally dressed musicians, and the glittering chandeliers, the walls were raw lumber and the ceiling was covered with nailed-on panels of embossed tin painted white. Evidently Anderson had thrown the place up as fast as he could, leaving wallpaper and such truck for later, if ever. Judging by the crowd at the bar and at the tables with which the floor was jammed—only a few occupied by ordinary drinkers, the rest devoted to poker, faro, and chuckaluck—every day of operation meant considerable money for Anderson.

Butch's glance roved back toward the balcony, then stopped. In the wall just above it he saw a small, square opening and in it a portion of a face. His eyebrows lifted.

He turned to the barkeep and paid him for the whiskey. "I was just sort of wondering—what's up there?" He nodded toward the balcony and second floor.

"Rooms," the bartender said.

Rooms. The place didn't look much like a hotel at all, for sure. . . .

The bartender pointed down the bar at a scrawny girl in a low-cut dress that revealed little of interest; she seemed to have had the smallpox—or some pox— once. "If you want to satisfy your curiosity, give her ten bucks. She'll show you one of 'em."

The girl smiled at Butch, adding bad teeth to the roster of her visible charms.

"I'm not *that* curious," he muttered, and returned to his drink. A close survey of the room raised some interesting questions. Such as, why was the fiddler in the band watching the room so closely? And especially, why was there a six-gun visible through the front of his tailcoat?

And the chuckaluck dealer out on the floor—armed, too. Now that Butch was looking for them, he could see holstered revolvers all over the place, on dealers and players alike. And one empty holster . . .

His eyes sharpened and he stooped unobtrusively to get a better look. An empty holster meant there was a drawn gun someplace, unless the owner had been careless or unlucky—yes, there it was in the hand of the clean-cut young fellow playing poker, pointing under the table at the three other players and obviously out of their sight. He whistled soundlessly. The kid seemed to like to play cards with an ace in the hole, for sure. This could be *some* kind of a lively evening. . . .

Longabaugh studied his cards. A lousy hand, not that it mattered.

The heavyset man across from him, the big winner so far, looked at him impatiently, then at the pile of coins and bills in the center of the table. "It's up to you. What do you say?"

Longabaugh looked at the cards for a moment, then said quietly, "I'm holding a gun under the table—now, *don't* do anything dumb. Just keep acting like we're playin' cards here."

The heavyset man's eyes bulged and he tensed in his chair, but kept silent. The two other players glanced around nervously but made no move.

"Okay, good," Longabaugh said. "Just keep playing. Now I'm gonna raise a hundred." He nodded toward the man on his left. "And you are gonna see me and *raise* me another hundred. An' we'll just keep going round the table until you've put all your money in the pot. You got that?" The others gave reluctant nods. "Okay, *one* hundred."

He slid his money to join the pile on the table.

"Well, okay," the man on his left said nervously. "A . . . a hundred. An' I'll raise you two. Hell, *five*— let's get this over with!"

The heavyset man glared when his turn came, but added his contribution. But when the "play" came around to him again, he squinted at Longabaugh and said, "You're bluffing."

"Well, let's see if I am," Longabaugh said pleasantly. He studied his hand. "I've got a pair of threes and—" his right hand was out of sight beneath the table, but the heavyset man could see the arm tense "—five bullets aiming at your belly."

The heavyset man glared again, then lowered his eyes. Longabaugh relaxed and contentedly watched the pile of money grow. This spectacle was sufficiently absorbing for him not to notice when the orchestra trailed off in mid-tune, and the noise of the slap of cards, boisterous laughter, and the clinking of bottles and glasses began to die away. Nor was he aware of the gun-toting violinist's sudden sharp look and the quick rap on the balcony above him he gave with his bow.

But when the quiet became absolute, Longabaugh did look around, to find what seemed to be every eye in the room focused on him—especially those of two unfriendly-looking men who had just emerged onto the balcony, carrying rifles.

He laid his cards down and reached for the pot, giving his fellow players the broad smile of the gentlemanly winner who regrets having wiped his opponents out and would be glad to give them a chance to get even but has this policy about not taking IOUs, and in any case is faced with a pressing engagement elsewhere. . . .

He kept his eyes on the surly, heavyset man, whose face was dangerously dark—but it was the two quiet men on either side of him who suddenly grabbed the table and upended it toward him.

Longabaugh dove for the floor, hit, rolled, and fired two shots upward. The rope holding the chandelier at the rear of the room parted; gamblers and drinkers shouted and scattered as the fixture slammed into the floor with the sound of a hundred broken windows and sent tongues of flaming kerosene across the raw wood.

One of the riflemen on the balcony raised his weapon to his shoulder and sighted down into the melee.

"Forgit it," his companion said. "You can't get a clear shot, and Anderson'll be mad as hell if you ventilate one of the payin' customers—hell an' damnation!"

"Madder'n he's gonna be now?" the first rifleman said with gloomy satisfaction. Another shot from Longabaugh had sent the remaining chandelier crashing down. The saloon was now in near-darkness, the only illumination being provided by flames from the spilled kerosene, and that waning by the second as hoarsely shouting men trampled on the burning fuel.

"Looks some like pictures of Hell I seen once in a book," one of the baffled riflemen said. "About this feller that went there for a look-see."

"Dumb-fool kind of thing to do," the other man said, looking at the wild scene below and conscious that there wasn't a damn thing he could do about it. "Bad enough to git *sent* there. A man'd have to be plain loco to pay a visit deliberate."

"I dunno. I've knowed fellers that out of their own choice went to Dodge City."

Longabaugh, near the door, was confronted by four shadowy figures; the flickering light gleamed off the barrels of their drawn guns. He snapped off two shots, scattering them; then the hammer clicked on an empty chamber. He spun and grabbed at the waist of a man prudently leaning against the bar and taking no part in the turmoil, felt the heft of a revolver butt, and snatched it from its holder.

"Hey!" Butch said indignantly. "That's a brand-new gun!"

"Good," Longabaugh muttered. "Then it oughta work." He tested this proposition with a fusillade directed at the riflemen on the balcony which sent them diving for cover. Now other men were moving in from both sides—any second, he thought, they'd see a way to get a clear shot.

He bent low and leaped through a window in the wall next to the bar. It was not open, and a scatter of sash and glass sprayed out as he hit the ground and ran. Butch, crowding to the window for a better look—and, as it happened, jostling the arm of a man who was trying to get off a shot at the fleeing Longabaugh—saw him bounding through the night, the window's net curtains tangled about his head and flowing behind him like an incongruous bridal veil.

"*Get the marshal!*" a maddened voice bayed. "Get some light in here! Get back to your tables, dealers! Get the hell *going,* all o' you!"

A few candles and pine knots had restored the lighting to about a twentieth the level once provided by the wrecked chandeliers, but enough for Butch to see a tall man in a black coat waving his arms and shouting in the center of the floor. Anderson himself, obviously.

Butch wandered over to him and inquired, "Getting up a posse?"

Anderson said, "Damn right! Them chandeliers was my pride an' joy, shipped in from San Francisco. Soon's Marshal Le Fors gets here, I'm saddling and riding out with him after that hyderphobia skunk. Need some more men—you game, stranger?"

Butch nodded. "Surest thing you know. The sonofabitch stole my gun!" But he could not repress a half-smile, fortunately hidden in the dimness. That kid had showed a lot of nerve and style. Very damned little in the brains line, though.

CHAPTER THREE

Butch reined his horse to a stop, lifted his damp hat and took a swipe at his sweaty forehead. He reached for his canteen, then decided against it. This tracking was hot work, and it'd be best to save the water for when it was really needed. With this marshal in charge of things, it could be a long job.

Le Fors, off his horse at the head of the file, was hunched over by the edge of a small stream that ran through the grove of aspens where they had halted. The flat white straw hat he wore was tilted at an angle indicating that he was studying the ground closely. Butch grimaced. The damn man was a human bloodhound—he'd picked up traces of their quarry on rocky ground as well as any Indian tracker could have, even the legendary Lord Baltimore, and was clearly going to follow him as far as he could, no matter that the rest of the posse were saddle-sore and beginning to wonder what was so wonderful about being out after an armed and remarkably reckless hardcase.

Having a fellow like old Ray Bledsoe on your trail, that was one thing—he got you or you got away, one or the other. But this Le Fors . . . he seemed like some kind of machine: set him going to catch a man, and he'd just keep at it, as if he wasn't built to do anything else. A man on the dodge with Le Fors after him would feel pretty jumpy, never knowing when that white skimmer would show up in his back trail. . . .

Le Fors remounted and sent his horse halfway across the stream, then stopped and leaned forward, looking hard at the opposite bank.

One of Anderson's rifle-toters, sporting a deputy's star, left the side of his weary-looking employer and rode to where Le Fors's horse stood in midstream. "Something wrong, Mr. Le Fors?"

"He didn't cross here," the marshal said slowly.

"Then those *aren't* his tracks you been following?" The deputy looked back anxiously toward Anderson. The saloonkeeper wouldn't care at all for having spent half a day on a wild-goose chase; and, since he had no inclination to brace Le Fors about that, would for certain work off his bad temper on the nearest man on his payroll—which was the deputy.

"Those are his tracks, all right," Le Fors said, to the deputy's relief. "He just didn't cross. There's none on the other side. He rode up the stream bed here."

The marshal turned his horse upstream and splashed through the shallow water, leaning over his mount's side.

"How d'ya know?" the deputy asked.

"His horse kicked the pebbles over right here." Le Fors pointed. "See how there's moss on top of the others?"

He raised his right hand and brought it forward in the classic "move on" gesture, and urged his horse ahead. The seven other members of the posse followed in single file. Butch, bringing up the rear, wondered, as he had through much of the chase, if it made sense for him to be here. His plan had come to him as a beautifully logical inspiration when Le Fors had set up the posse last night, but after a night and part of the morning on the trail, it seemed less convincing. Maybe it would have been better to stay back in Steamboat Springs—maybe pick up a few dollars helping repair the damage to Anderson's place, and be on his way. But . . . hell, one way or another, this excursion could prove mighty interesting.

The stream bank shallowed as the posse emerged into a clearing in the mountain woods. Ahead lay a steep slope, almost treeless, studded with crags and boulders, flat at the top. It struck Butch forcibly that up to forty men could lie concealed there, completely invisible from where the posse stood, bunched up now for conference.

"He's up there," Le Fors said, pointing toward the summit of the hill.

"How d'ya figure that?" Butch said.

"Well," the marshal said, "he's been riding all night, so his horse's gotta be tired." He ticked off that point on one long forefinger, then tapped the next one. "On the other side of there there's nothing but desert. He wouldn't be fool enough to try an' cross *that* by day. Plus—"a third finger registered the final argument, "—a spot like that gives him a great position."

"Against us," one of the riders said thoughtfully.

"We've got numbers on our side," Le Fors said, surveying his posse. "We can *afford* to lose a few. Let's go in and get him."

Anderson and the other Steamboat Springers might not have been especially quick thinkers, but it was clear to Butch that they were doing fast calculations about how many "a few" from eight left, and didn't care for the answer, or for the prospect of being one of those subtracted.

"Uh . . ." said the rider who had spoken. "We don't think he did nothin' so turble we got to take him in for it, Mr. Le Fors."

"You're afraid to go in there," Le Fors said, with the air of a man who had just turned over a rock and found what might be expected underneath it—no real scorn or disgust, but a glum acceptance that there were people who would let the prospect of getting shot deter them from a manhunt.

Anderson spoke up, shrugging. "He did a little damage to my saloon. A lotta the boys shoot the place up now an' then." Butch gave a quick grin. The slaughtered chandeliers' cries for vengeance seemed to ring a lot less loudly in Anderson's ears than they had the night before.

Le Fors looked at him coldly. "I can't go in there and get him alone."

"No, you can't, Mr. Le Fors," Anderson assured him. "It'd be suicide."

Le Fors turned to his deputy. "Then it's up to us."

"Us?" the deputy said wonderingly, as if the marshal had addressed him in French or Choctaw. Then he gave a sigh, unpinned his badge, placed it in Le Fors's hand, and, to emphasize his retirement from public life, backed his horse until it stood next to Anderson's.

Le Fors looked around at the rest of the posse. He held the badge up; it caught the sunlight and glinted. "Anybody want to wear this?"

No one said "no" aloud; but lowered eyes and almost imperceptible shakes of heads gave the answer clearly enough.

Le Fors looked at them with contempt and spurred his horse forward, then halted it in the middle of the clearing. Quieting the animal, which seemed no more at ease in the open than members of the recently retired posse, he called up toward the seemingly untenanted hillside.

"Seems they don't want you as bad as I do." His shout was amplified by echoes from the boulders. "So I'll have to get you *next* time around! I'll see you again. Try and remember my face . . . *the name's Le Fors!*"

He held his hat away from his head and stood high in his stirrups, giving the unseen watcher a full view. Then he settled into the saddle, jammed the hat savagely onto his head, and sent the horse cantering out of the clearing and back into the woods.

"Well," Anderson said after a moment. "I guess we ain't doing any good here, boys. Time to get on back to town. I appreciate your . . . um, what you done. Drinks on the house, tonight."

The riders mumbled their thanks, but took their departure in a cloud of shamed gloom, keeping their eyes front and down. It was for this reason that none of them noticed for some time that the last man in line was not with them; and none of them gave a damn when they did. Being a stranger, he was likely to have a looser tongue about what had gone on in the clearing than any of the townsmen, and that, they felt, they could comfortably do without.

Butch, alone in the clearing, dismounted and tied his horse to a tree. Keeping a wary eye on the rocky slope, he walked toward it, stopping at a point halfway between the trees and the first tumbled rocks.

"Hey?" he called. There was no answer but a faint *ey-ey* echoing back.

"Listen! If you're up there . . . I'm the one whose gun you took last night. I had to buy myself another new one. Twelve *dollars*."

. . . llars.

"Look, I want to talk to you." He waited for a moment, aware of being hot and thirsty . . . and of hearing nothing.

"Listen, I'll tell you what. I'm gonna put my new gun down right on this rock *here*." He laid the weapon down. "See, no gun." He raised both hands and made a slow turn. A spot squarely between his shoulder blades suddenly seemed to him to have a bull's-eye painted on it in glaring colors, but . . .

"Okay?" He was facing the hill again now, and put his hands down.

"Listen, I'm here because I want to do you a *favor*." If I am making a fool of myself talking to a pile of rocks, he thought, I don't know as I can stand it; I'll have to kick myself clear back to Steamboat—

37

"I'm doing *you* one right now."

Butch jumped at the sound of the voice—not shouting at all, and *damned* close. "How?" he called, lowering his voice.

"By not pulling the trigger," the disembodied voice informed him.

Butch considered this for a moment, then said, somewhat flatly, "Right." He brightened and stepped toward the rocks as he went on, "See, and I don't figure you *will*, because—"

An echoing explosion, a puff of rock dust to his left, and the spiteful whine of a ricocheting slug indicated that Butch had miscalculated. He stopped dead.

"Hey, you got nothing to fear from me," he called plaintively.

"*I* know that," the voice said in reasonable tones.

Butch sighed and held his hands a little up and out from his body, enough to show that he was a peaceable fellow and couldn't mean any harm to anybody, even a suspicious hardcase with a ready gun. Seemed to work pretty well, that gun; pity, Butch thought, that he'd never had a chance to try it out. He began, very slowly, advancing up the slope toward the rock from behind which the voice had seemed to come.

"Listen, I'm an outlaw, too," he said. "That's why I followed you. Only I'm a really lousy tracker, so I figured I'd join up with that posse and see what *they* could do about finding you. And here I am. You gotta admit *that's* smart."

The rock was only a few yards ahead of him now.

From behind it the voice said unemotionally, "Or dumb." Butch heard the unmistakable click of a revolver's hammer being pulled back to full cock.

Butch swallowed and stopped. It was hot, out here in the open with the sun bouncing off bare rocks, but he felt distinctly chilly. It struck him that if a fellow could arrange it so as to be scared silly often enough during the hot weather, it would be as good as ducking into an icehouse for getting cool. Might be some money in hiring out to do that—for a small fee, Butch Cassidy will personally put you in fear of your life, relieving you from the effects of high temperatures and possibly preventing heatstroke. . . . This was an awfully grim-looking place to die . . . but then, there wasn't anything so great about dying in a *pretty* place, come to think of it. He'd come this far, and it was time to see if his idea had been as good as he thought or if he'd finally run out of luck.

"If you kill me," he said, "you'll never know about my favor." He tensed. Put that way, it didn't seem like all that much of an argument. If he'd had the misfortune to take out after someone like Billy the Kid or John Wesley Hardin, a fellow who'd rather shoot you than shake your hand, then it was curtains for Butch Cassidy. But he was betting the other way—betting, it occurred to him, quite a lot; his whole life was in the pot, and it was up to the other fellow to see him, raise, or fold.

A crumpled hat appeared slowly from behind the rock, then the face of the kid he'd seen last night buying into the poker game with a gun, then more of the kid, then the gun itself—no, *not* the ace-in-the-hole six-shooter he'd used then, but Butch's own purchase of the day before, damn it. He drills me, it won't cost him a cent, Butch reflected gloomily. Butch Cassidy will go down in legend, song and story as the only outlaw that ever financed his own demise, bullets and all. It was a mighty impressive weapon, seen from this end, and, looking straight down the barrel as he was, it was no trouble at all to calculate where a slug fired from it would wind up.

The gun barrel flicked to the right. "Up," the kid said. "You first."

Butch lowered his hands and began to walk up the slope ahead of the kid. Soon he had to scramble among the scattered rocks, grabbing at some of the more solidly anchored ones for support. Behind him he could hear the noises of the kid's progress. He glanced back. As he had suspected, the gun was still trained on him.

"You want to use both hands, a climb like this," he called. "If you was to slip or something, that gun might go off."

"I don't mind that," the kid said. "Keep moving."

"Oh, well. It's your gun." Now, anyhow, Butch added to himself. But it's my back that any accidents would happen to, not that I suppose that'd cut much ice with him.

He continued climbing until he pulled himself over the edge of the mesa that topped the hill. Nearly flat as a floor, covered with scattered rocks and a few stunted trees, it was about fifty feet across. At the far side a horse stood tethered to a tree, well out of sight from the woods below. Next to it lay a pair of saddle-bags and a bedroll.

"Home, sweet home," Butch observed as the kid followed him onto the mesa. There was no reply. The kid, turning as he walked, to keep the revolver trained on Butch, went to the saddlebags, squatted, and rummaged in them.

He withdrew two tin plates, a battered cardboard box, and two spoons. One-handed, he filled one plate with a mound of dry cereal and moved several feet away. He sat on a rock and began to wolf down the cereal.

Leaving the other plate and spoon and the cereal there wasn't exactly a case of "Welcome, stranger, and dig in, there's plenty for all," but it did constitute some sort of invitation, Butch figured. And it would be wise to accept it. For one thing, he was damned hungry; the posse's provisioning arrangements had been hasty and scanty. For another, a man you'd shared a meal with might be less likely to plug you.

He poured some cereal into the plate, and took it and the spoon to a boulder near the kid. The gun barrel moved. "Over there."

Butch moved to another rock, about ten feet from the kid, and sat down. Maybe he's afraid I'll snitch some from his plate when he isn't looking, he told himself morosely. Fat chance. He rubbed the spoon clean on his shirt, trying not to be too conspicuous about it; no sense in making a point of criticizing his host's housekeeping.

He dug into the cereal, which immediately gave him the sensation of having taken in a mouthful of sawdust. With a little condensed milk and sugar, the stuff would have been bearable, but the kid's larder didn't seem to provide for luxuries.

"I'll bet this is even better hot," he called, after he had got down the first mouthful—except for some fragments that seemed to have lodged in his windpipe.

The kid ignored him and continued eating, bolting the cereal down as if it were as good as broiled buffalo hump, or at least a plate of beans.

"I'm Butch Cassidy. Maybe you've heard of me?"

The kid, jaws working, still holding the gun pointed at Butch, regarded him impassively.

"Maybe not," Butch said. "You got a name?"

The kid swallowed the remainder of his mouthful and said, "Uh-huh." He dug his spoon into the diminishing heap of cereal and took on another load.

This fellow seems to be ready to chase Ray Bledsoe for the silence prize, Butch thought. Like pulling teeth to get a word out of him.

"You shoot good," he ventured.

"That the favor? Telling me that?"

"I'm getting to it!" Butch said. He set down his plate and leaned forward. "The way you shot your way outta that spot last night was really something special, so it was."

41

The kid received the compliment with the same lack of reaction he had displayed throughout the conversation.

"But you wouldn't have gotten *into* that spot unless you were pretty dumb."

The kid stopped chewing. His eyes narrowed, and, even from ten feet away, Butch could see his forefinger tightening on the revolver's trigger.

"You've gotta admire my honesty," Butch said nervously.

"The hell I do."

Butch wished fervently that he had had a chance to try out the gun before passing it on to its new owner. Unless the trigger action was pretty stiff, he was about a feather-touch away from being a gone goose. But now he was into it, and the only thing to do was go on. And make it *damn* good. "Trying to rob a game in a casino full of people . . . that's just stupid."

Not as stupid, maybe, he suddenly realized, as telling a few home truths to a hair-trigger-tempered outlaw with the drop on you: the kid's gun lifted and centered on Butch's forehead.

"*Okay*," he said placatingly, "maybe not *stupid*, maybe that's the wrong word, but a man who can handle a gun like you shouldn't be eating cold cereal out in the middle of nowhere." He took in a deep breath and let it out. The gun hadn't moved, and the kid still looked unfriendly, but the situation wasn't getting any worse just yet. "Now, here's the favor I'm gonna do you. I'm gonna show you the *right* way to rob a casino. Then after that, I figure . . . you . . . and me—you know, together—could pull off a lot of stuff. You being good at what you're good at . . . me bein' good at what I'm good at."

"What're *you* good at?" the kid asked with genuine, if unflattering, interest.

"Thinking, planning, stuff like that." *Sure*, Cassidy. You planned yourself into this setup, right? Not too many men besides Butch Cassidy could go out after a partner and wind up with every chance of dying with a mouth coated with cereal. "I'm as good at using my head as you are with that gun," he said earnestly.

The kid looked at him intently for a moment, then shook his head. "I work alone."

Irritation at the kid's obstinacy flashed through Butch. A chance to team up with one of the real thinkers in the thieving line, and he was treating it as if it were a pile of buffalo chips. "You're *real* successful at it, too, I've noticed," he said.

He regretted his comment immediately. The kid jumped up from his seat, his eyes wide and glaring, his face set. He was still ten feet away from Butch, but his outstretched arm with the gun at the end of it seemed to reach out to cover most of the distance between them. Butch thought he could almost see the cylinder starting to turn, bringing the loaded chamber under the raised hammer. But the gun was no more alarming than the whole picture the kid presented. He was like a weapon himself, hair-trigger murder embodied.

"I could drop you right *here*!" the kid shouted. "I could put a *bullet* through your head right now an' nobody'd ever know, so don't you be telling me how dumb I am! I'm as smart as you are, you *hear* me?"

Butch did, and a good deal louder than he liked. Okay, this deal had gone sour, and it was time to lay down the hand and walk away from it. Anyhow, if the kid was going to go off like a Gatling every time anybody gave him a little friendly criticism, it'd never have worked out. Mustering what jauntiness he could, he said ironically, "With that in your hand, you're a damn *genius*."

Lifting his hands high, he stood, turned his back on the kid, and walked to the edge of the mesa. It was hard to get down the slope with any dignity, but Butch did what he could, always conscious of his former weapon trained on his back.

At the bottom of the slope he headed for the clearing where his horse still stood.

"You're forgettin' something, Mister Planner." Butch looked back toward the hilltop and saw the kid's figure against the sky. One hand held the revolver high and waved it derisively, the other pointed at a spot somewhere to Butch's left.

Butch cursed and retraced his steps to the rock on which he had laid his new gun. Anybody, he told himself, could have overlooked a detail like that, what with all that had been going on; and likely he wouldn't have gone more than a hundred yards or so before he recalled it. But it made one hell of an advertisement for his talents as a mastermind. . . .

CHAPTER FOUR

Green River may well be green along its upper reaches, before Horse Creek, the Pineys, Sandy Creek, Slate Creek, and Muddy Creek have added their influences; but by the time it courses through Lodore Canyon in Utah it is reddish-brown, a variant on the color of the bizarre rock formations that surround it. These, carved by water and wind for tens of millions of years, are uncanny and spectacular, sometimes displaying the fossilized bones of creatures the Indians and early mountain men puzzled at and preferred not to think about. The area was dramatic enough to deserve an impressive name, the Devil's Opera House, say; but historical accident had dealt with it prosaically, making it known to all and sundry simply as Brown's Hole.

On the outlaw trail that ran from nearly to the Canadian border to Mexico, Brown's Hole was a major station. Like the Hole in the Wall to the north and Robber's Roost, three hundred miles south, it combined the virtues of water and grazing land with remoteness and remarkable defensibility. Rustled cattle could wax fat, and hard-working felons could go about their work, rest, and recreations without unfeeling interference from marshals, sheriffs, and the like. The Hole took in parts of Colorado, Wyoming, and Utah, giving lawmen of each of the three states the excuse of jurisdictional uncertainty to pass up the chance of picking their way down the steep trails to the valley to serve warrants on well-armed and notably short-

45

tempered men, all of them surrounded by hardcases of equal caliber.

The storekeeper-postmaster at Bridgeport, at the Utah end of Brown's Hole, was used to a more varied clientele than most of his colleagues. The people who entered and left the Hole traded with him, to his considerable profit, and he knew enough to keep his mouth shut about their affairs and not to display surprise or interest at anything they might let drop. It had been made clear to him a long time ago that a discreet man in his position would prosper, and that a loose-tongued one would be soon silenced.

"No mail for Parker," he told Butch. "George *or* Robert."

"Santiago Maxwell?"

"Don't believe so . . . no."

"Cassidy?"

The storekeeper pawed in the *C* pigeonhole in the post-office area of his establishment. "Nothin' *for* any Cassidy, but somethin' *about* a Mike Cassidy—a circular, some sheriff or so would like to talk some things over with him. But that wouldn't be you, judgin' by the age an' other particulars, not that I'd be interested in takin' any notice of that, anyhow, you'll understand."

So old Mike's wanted, Butch thought. Nothing new for him, that's for sure. Be a damn shame if they get him . . . wasn't for him, I wouldn't have this trade, or this name.

"Ah . . . anything for Ingerfield?" None of the people who'd known him under that alias would be likely to want to write him, or know that he might be asking for mail at the last stop before Brown's Hole, but no harm in asking.

"That there ain't," the storekeeper said, without checking the *I* pigeonhole. "Ingerfield's a name I'd remember. As much," he added hastily, "as I remember *anything*, names and such. So many fellers go through here, a man can't keep track of 'em. Ten minutes from now, was somebody to ask me who'd been in here, askin' for what mail, I 'spect it'd of gone clean out of my mind, as I could state on my Bible oath." A man who expected letters as George or Robert Parker, Cassidy, Maxwell, or Ingerfield, it seemed to him, was a man who should have it made clear to him that his aliases were of no concern whatever to a hard-working storekeeper. Only last Tuesday he had handed over a letter claimed by a man identifying himself as Grover Cleveland, without indicating by word or gesture that it was anything out of the way for the President of the United States to be picking up his mail in a remote Utah store, or that the President, seen in the flesh, should prove to be a short, swarthy man with a bad knife scar traversing his face. The customer says he's Cleveland, Cleveland he is. *Or* Parker, (G. or R.), Maxwell, Cassidy, or Ingerfield.

"Well, no mail for you, Mister . . . ah, sir," the storekeeper said. "Sorry about that. Anything else I can do for you? I got a new line of relish in, good with meats an' savories."

"What's a savory?" Butch asked.

"I dunno, that's what it says on the label, for meats an' savories. But it'd be the meats you're interested in, I'd say—down there in the Hole, I 'spect beef's a pretty regular item on the menu, eh? Meanin' nothin' *by* that, you understand, but it's well known that there's lots of, um, ranchers in there, all with good reputations, as I have many a time been glad to tell anyone as might come askin' about such."

"I'm not in the ranching line," Butch said.

"*Ah*," the storekeeper said, breaking into a light sweat. It would be only polite to ask this frank-faced young fellow what he did for a living, given this opening. And, given the class of people who patronized his store—and, even more important, given the six-gun at this man's waist—such a question could also be fatal.

"I got transportation and financial interests," Butch said. "Many opportunities for the forward-looking man in railroads, banking, things like that, if you know how to take advantage of them."

The storekeeper recovered something of his former aplomb. *That* Cassidy: the Denver & Rio Grande train robbery seven years back; the Denver First National Bank (a classic: Cassidy to the bank president: "I've just overheard a plan to rob your bank." President: "My God: how do you know about this plot?" Cassidy: "Because I planned it. Hands up!") ; the San Miguel Bank in Telluride. A deplorable citizen, no doubt, though a small-timer still, but his reputation was for nonviolence—no indication, so far, that he'd actually *shot* anyone. If this Cassidy was settling into Brown's Hole for a spell, there'd likely be some interesting reading in the *Salt Lake Herald* before long.

Declining the relish, Butch bought a few cans of condensed milk and of beans, coffee, sugar, and a slab of bacon. Surveying his shrunken bankroll, he realized that he'd damn *soon* have to start looking after his . . . transportation and financial interests. He could expect to find some nervy fellows in the Hole, but nobody of outstanding quality. . . .

Picking his way along the trail that led down the nearly sheer slope of the Lodore to the valley of the Green River—impossible to find from the more traveled ways of the area unless you'd been told just what signs to look for—Butch brooded over the problem of finding a good partner. A man could have all the plans in the world, but they weren't worth spit unless he had the manpower to back them up. O.C., Harve Logan, Elza Lay, Bill Carver—they were handy enough with their six-shooters, but there wasn't anything special about them; they could work out okay on one job, then pull some bonehead play on the next that would ruin the whole thing. Like Al Rainer. If Al hadn't just *had* to have his mail, and asked that girl

48

to fetch it from town for him, Ray Bledsoe would never have trailed her to the hideout and taken them. And after messing things up, Al had somehow been found not guilty, and it had been Butch who had done the time. Maybe, Butch reflected, they'd figured it was a good idea to leave a knothead like Al on the loose. Anytime he got involved in a job, it'd be easy enough to round up anyone else who'd been in on it.

If only that kid who'd tried to rob the game at Anderson's hadn't been so much on the prod that he couldn't listen to reason . . .

Preoccupied with these reflections, Butch did not notice a glint of sunlight from a pair of field glasses trained on him from the canyon rim. Far above him, a tall man in work clothes and a battered hat lowered the glasses and nodded to the men with him, then set his horse toward the hidden entrance to the trail.

Picking his way along the narrow track that ran beside the river, Butch stiffened in the saddle at the sound of hoofs on stone just ahead. Around a sharp bend in the trail another horse and rider appeared, and Butch relaxed. The other man, cold-eyed, with a fleshy nose and a full, drooping moustache, let his hand slide toward the gun at his side, then withdrew it and gave Butch a snaggle-toothed grin.

"Hiya, Butch."

The trail was so narrow at this point that both men's horses had to step carefully in order to squeeze by each other.

"Hello, Harvey." Butch, almost face to face with him, sized him up. Harve Logan had a sight of good work to his credit, but wasn't so hot at following a plan. He always made the mistake of thinking he could figure things out better than the fellow whose business it was, and that meant a lot of time wasted in showing him who was boss.

"I was lookin' for ya," Logan said. "Mint train come through a couple weeks ago, loaded with money, but I couldn't find ya to help rob it." He evidently did not consider any conversation he might have with Butch worth stopping for, as he kept his horse moving.

"I've been in prison for a year," Butch said.

Logan, now down the trail a few paces behind Butch, called, "Guess *that's* why I couldn't find ya."

"Probably it," Butch muttered. That was the class of thinking Harve usually displayed. Butch made a mental note that any future plans calling for Harve's services should be simple and easily explainable.

The storekeeper felt unhappy. This fellow's gun wasn't actually out, and his hand wasn't even hovering near the butt, but there was something about him that suggested he could have it drawn, aimed, and emptied in about nothing flat. One thing, he didn't look like a lawman, like that bunch that had gone through this morning, so it might be safe to be a *little* informative . . .

"I wouldn't know about *names*," he said, "but a feller somethin' like the one you're talkin' about might of come through here not so long ago. Chance he might be visitin' some acquaintances in Brown's Hole—or, of course, maybe not. I don't follow folks' business at all close, you understand."

The stranger nodded. "Good. He ain't been here, I ain't been here, and you ain't noticed anything. I'll be on my way now."

"Um," the storekeeper said. "If you ain't familiar with these parts, I don't know as you'd want to try to find your way down into Brown's Hole. The fellers there is some touchy about visitors and they don't mark the trails so good. Easy to get lost . . ."

The stranger grinned wolfishly. "I ain't been lost, strayed, or stolen yet that I know of. And as for them folks being touchy—well, I generally manage to make myself as welcome most places as I wanna be."

The storekeeper nodded. He didn't see anyone inviting this hombre to hit the trail before it suited him, any more than you'd want to suggest to a cougar that it was time to move on from its kill.

The struggling calf rolled its eyes and bawled angrily as the red-hot iron approached its side. It had experienced this once before and had not cared for it at all. The glowing metal hovered above the two short horizontal lines branded on the animal's hide, then dipped down; the calf yelled and a stench of burned hair and flesh arose. The two lines were still there when the iron was withdrawn, but were now surrounded by a circle and joined by a line running from the left end of the lower line to the right end of the top one.

"See, nothin' to it," said the beefy, crop-haired man who held the iron. He straightened as he spoke, looming above the men around him. O.C. Hanks was known to have killed several men, and there were rumors that he had done one in simply by sitting on him, hard. Given O.C.'s heft, this was possible, and there had been several lively discussions—conducted well out of O.C.'s hearing—about just what he would notch to remind him of that victim. His small eyes squinted as he surveyed the motley crew of pupils. "That Lazy Eleven critter is now part of the good ol' Circle Z. Okay, boys, let's see you try it."

Hanks shook his head as two weedy youths wrestled another calf to the ground. "Naw, that's the wrong—" he started to call, but stopped as the man he had been about to advise took a flailing hoof squarely between the legs and abandoned his task in order to fall to the ground, curl up like a hoop snake, cup his hands about the stricken area, drum his heels on the earth, and emit a shrill, steady whining noise.

An eager replacement grabbed the calf's leg and held it. With the animal at least partly secured, another reached for the branding iron, which Hanks had returned to the fire after his demonstration. Hanks opened his mouth to shout a warning, but was again forestalled as the cowboy screamed and dropped the iron, dancing around and flapping his seared hand.

Hanks shook his head and closed his eyes. "One ain't got the sense to guard his fambly jewels," he muttered, "and t'other b'lieves he c'n pick up red-hot arn barehanded." It seemed to him, contemplating his recruits, that he could have made a more effective rustler out of two sticks and a potato peeling than one of these fellows.

Butch, enjoying the easy riding along the stretch of grassland after the tough going through the canyon, observed the cowboys' mishaps and grinned. O.C. would be mad as a bear with a sore paw.

He reined up behind the huge man, dismounted, and approached him. "Hello, O.C."

Hanks did not turn. Butch snapped his fingers in exasperation, then moved around to Hank's other side; he'd forgotten O.C. was deaf as a post in his left ear. Again, "Hello, O.C."

Hanks spun around. His huge face lit up. "Butch!" He grabbed Butch's hand and pumped it. "Jesus, am I glad to see *you*."

"Glad to see you, too, O.C."

Hanks looked at the inept cowboys still struggling with the calf, and shook his head. As if to emphasize the fact that he considered himself off duty now, he buttoned the shapeless vest he wore over a dirty wool shirt—buttoned the one button he could, the garment having been made with someone built to a more normal scale in mind.

They walked back toward where Butch's horse stood. "You should *see* what's been driftin' in here nowadays," Hanks said mournfully. S'posed to be outlaws, they say . . . rustlers. Well, they ain't." He jerked a meaty thumb backward over his shoulder. "Just kids mostly, dumber'n shit."

He stopped and looked closely at Butch. "Hey," he said, "I thought that judge over in Lander give you two years. You're out early, ain't ya?"

Butch hesitated. If word of his promise got around, he'd lose considerable face with this crowd. Or worse, they'd insist on his breaking it as soon as possible, pulling off some job in Wyoming just to show he hadn't gone soft. O.C. and the others would be bound to feel that an outlaw who kept his word to the authorities couldn't be trusted. "I made a deal," he said finally.

"What kinda deal?"

"A deal, that's all," Butch said shortly. He caught his horse's reins and started for the hillside at the edge of the pasture. Hanks followed, looking at him curiously.

The steep trail up the hillside hadn't changed in the year he'd been away, and his cabin, when he got to it, looked the same as it had when he'd left. It wasn't much, but moss and clay jammed in gaps between the logs kept the wind out and, protected by the massive rock ledge that overhung it, the cabin was sheltered from the worst of the snow. After the Laramie pen, it looked comfortingly homelike. Butch tied his horse's reins to a post, opened the cabin door, and stopped in the doorway.

He wondered for a wild second if the cabin might not have been dislodged by a storm and rolled down the hillside, then been returned to its place by kind friends who had not bothered to do anything about its contents. That would go *some* way toward explaining the state it was in. . . .

"Butch?" Hanks, puffing from the climb up the trail, stood behind him. "Me an' Emma've been usin' your place while you was gone. . . . Hope you don't mind."

Butch slowly looked over the interior of his cabin. Heaps of dirty clothes made islands on the floor; unwashed crockery, broken and whole, could be seen almost every place but the bare cupboard; the one chair lay on its side; the mattress, askew on the bed frame, was leaking straw; something that had once been a meal, too many days ago, was in a dish on the table. The effect might have been worse except for the drifts of dust that hid and softened some of the debris.

He stepped inside, Hanks following, and closed the door, dislodging a cloud of dust from the rafters.

"Hell, no," he said mildly. "It's nice to see a woman's touch around the place."

Hanks looked around, apparently seeing that his temporary quarters might not pass muster with a really finicky visitor. "She couldn't find the broom this mornin'," he muttered apologetically.

Butch removed his coat and hung it on a peg hammered into one wall. It was hard to know where to begin, but . . . He rummaged in a heap on the floor and withdrew a blanket. It was stained and stiff with grease; he firmly declined to wonder how it had got that way. He spread it on one of the few clear spaces on the floor and began piling things on it. No point in sorting out things now, he figured; get everything outside, souse the place down, and start over.

"Hey, really, Butch," Hanks said uneasily, "she'll get that." He brightened, grabbed a shirt, and began swiping it at the shelves and tabletop. This achieved mainly a more even distribution of the dust, settling it in the few places it had not yet found. Hanks's housecleaning also animated what Butch had taken for a particularly disreputable coat, which uncurled, raised itself on its three legs, bared stained teeth, and growled at Butch.

"Shut up, Ned," Hanks ordered his pet. "Good watchdog, never mind the missin' leg."

"Bet you haven't had anything stolen since you've had him," Butch said, folding the blanket around the miscellaneous assortment of debris he had loaded it with.

"Not that I *know* of." Hanks looked around the disordered cabin. "Hey, Butch, Emma'll be back soon. Make us some dinner."

"She *cooks*, too?" Butch lifted the blanket and staggered slightly as one foot skidded on something he didn't want to think about. "You're a lucky man, O.C."

"I *know*," Hanks said, beaming. He surveyed the results of his work complacently. He himself didn't mind if things were a bit rough and ready, but a finicky fellow like Butch was entitled to his own ways, too. This should be enough to satisfy him. "There," he said, giving a final swipe with the shirt and dropping it on the floor.

Butch carried the blanket-bundled junk outside and set it on the ground. As he straightened, he heard the sound of a fiddle scraping in the distance. "What's that?"

"We got us our own saloon now," Hanks said proudly from the doorway.

"Do tell," Butch said. "Brown's Hole's getting all civilized and currycombed, ain't it? Next thing, there'll be schools and stores and taxes."

Hanks shook his head. "I ain't heard no talk about such. Don't think I'd care for it, 'specially the taxes part."

"It'll be a while, I expect." Butch started back toward the cabin for another load, then stopped. "Listen, O.C., where'll you and Emma live now?"

"Been studyin' that out," Hanks said. "Harve Logan's got some business over Salt Lake way, left today—"

"Yeah," Butch said. "I passed him when I was coming in."

"—an' can't hardly be back inside of couple weeks. There's the business to do, an' the collectin' of the pay

55

for it, an' then some travelin' elsewheres on account of the posse, the business to be done involvin' a feller with a lot of friends."

"And one enemy," Butch said thoughtfully.

Hanks shrugged. "Anyhow, Harve's cabin's empty, an' I figured me an' Emma'd move our plunder in there until we c'n find somethin' more permanent. Harve'll be glad to have someone keepin' an eye on his place for him."

Butch grinned. "Sure he will." O.C. wasn't a mental giant, but you had to admit he was an original thinker. It would be hard to imagine anyone else who would entertain the proposition that Harvey Logan— "the infamous Kid Curry," the papers called him— would take kindly to the idea of having his quarters turned into a hog wallow by O.C. and his evidently well-matched Emma. But O.C. had got it into his head that Emma was a compendium of all the housewifely virtues, and once O.C.'s brain had taken hold of an idea, it hung onto it with a bear-trap grip.

"Why don't you go find Emma and tell her you're moving, get a start on it? That way you can be all settled in by night. I'll sort out this stuff and put yours to one side so's you can pick it up when you want."

"Okay," Hanks said slowly. "You wanna come an' have a meal with us?"

"I'd *admire* to," Butch said. "But my mama always told me you can't pay a call when someone moves in until after the lady of the house has her curtains up."

"That so?" O.C. said. "Well, I don't see that Emma'll be gettin' to that quite today. So . . ."

"So I'll get my stuff together and go on down to the saloon after dark, meet you there. I got some things I want to talk to you about."

Hanks shook his head. "Best we go there together. These new fellers that has come in won't know you, and they're still kind of spooked after that job we done on the Lazy Eleven a couple days back, might take a stranger for a lawman an' act accordin'. Be sorry for it afterward, but that wouldn't do you much good. Accourse," he added bitterly, "they'll git jumpy an' ready to slap leather if anyone farts sudden, but take sentry duty on the trails? Hafta practically *hogtie* 'em, an' even then I bet half of 'em go to sleep. Things ain't the way they was. But what I mean," he went on, "them kids bein' proddy an' foolish both, I better meet you down by the brandin' pen so's we can ride over there together, okay?"

"Okay, O.C." Butch waved as the massive man turned and started his scrambling descent down the trail, followed by the hobbling dog.

The big man in the battered hat peered through the field glasses into the gathering dusk and grunted. "There's a lookout on that knob over there. But he seems to of caught the sleepin' sickness or somethin', dozin' away comfortable as you please. We keep quiet, we can get by him without havin' to deal with him harsh and noisy."

The procession of mounted men moved silently along the rocky trail, the horses' hoofs wrapped in rags to muffle the sound of their passage.

CHAPTER FIVE

It had seemed to Butch that removing the traces of a year's occupation by Emma and O.C. would be about a year's job, if it could ever actually be done, so he was pleasantly surprised to find that it was only four hours before the cabin actually looked livable again. It was a little easier than he had expected to arrange things in an orderly manner, since a number of his utensils and dishes had perished or vanished, and items such as blankets and the mattress had been reduced to a state that made their disposal imperative.

By sunset, the only trace of O.C. and his lady was the heap of their belongings—some defying identification, but, Butch was sure, nothing he himself would *ever* have given house room to—in the patch of cleared ground in front of the cabin.

The evening chill had come on, and Butch shoved a few heavy chunks of split wood into the small rock fireplace, then some kindling. What he wanted was a slow fire, one that would just keep going while he was hoisting a few with O.C. and getting some business set up, and that he could build up high once he got back. When he had the wood arranged to his satisfaction, he struck a match on the rough rock of the fireplace and lit the whittled shavings that lay underneath the kindling.

After ten minutes, he was satisfied that the backlog had caught and would burn slowly enough to last out his absence. It was almost dark when he rode away;

looking back at the cabin, he was cheered at the sight of the dim glow of the fire through the lone window. It might not be much of a home, but it was something to come back to. Would have been a sight pleasanter if there was someone else there, but Mary—that whole side of his life—didn't belong in Brown's Hole. . . .

"It ain't much, but it's all we got," Hanks said, as he and Butch dismounted outside the log building. Music, talk, and a liquory atmosphere came from it; but that was about as far as any resemblance to Anderson's in Steamboat Springs went, Butch thought as he peered inside. Three whiskery fellows occupied the only chairs in the place, attacking a waltz tune Butch remembered as having something to do with a river over in Europe which was said to be beautiful and blue—probably no more of either, he suspected, than the Green was green—with a violin, a queer-looking cousin to a guitar, and a jug that gave off more or less tuneful mooing sounds when blown into.

A log plank supported by sawhorses held bottles of whiskey; behind it was an upright keg of beer. In front of it, a bunch of morose-looking young cowboys stood holding their drinks and sipping or gulping at them. Only one or two were saying anything. Maybe, Butch thought, they were music lovers and didn't want to break the spell. Or, from the way some of them were pouring the stuff down, maybe they were too drunk to talk. Or maybe again, they were natural non-conversers, being capable of thinking one step ahead of a cow, but not much beyond that. O.C. had rounded up a rare bunch, all right; could be he didn't want anyone smarter than he was working for him on a rustling job, which limited his choices considerably. Butch looked around the room but failed to see any familiar faces. Elza, Harve, Carver—none of them here. Then how in the hell was he ever going to put together any kind of useful organization? Face it, if

O.C. Hanks is the top of your pick, you're in trouble.

The ones who weren't standing and drinking and not talking were dancing and not talking. The sight of pairs of booted cowboys rotating in an approximation of a waltz did not strike Butch as particularly strange: with the life in such places as Brown's Hole tending to discourage the presence of women, anyone who felt the impulse to dance had to do it solo or with another man. Wasn't as if they *meant* anything by it . . .

"Next time you rustle something, O.C.," he murmured, "maybe it oughta be a bunch of women. These fellows might be able to handle 'em some better than they been doing with those cows you brought in."

"Hey, you!" Hanks shouted. "Music—shut up!"

The Blue Danube gurgled away into silence.

"This here's my buddy," Hanks informed the roomful of now attentive cowboys. "Butch Cassidy. Straight," he added impressively, like a master of ceremonies announcing that the attraction he is about to present has just entertained the crowned heads of Europe, "from the Wyoming State's Prison in Laramie. And I 'spect there's some of you yearling badmen will recall a withdrawal from the Denver National Bank not too long ago, not to mention the Denver an' Rio Grandy train job, 'bout which nothin' was ever *proved* against Butch, but . . ." He closed one eye and leered horribly. The fascinated audience murmured appreciatively.

Butch was stung. What was wrong with the San Miguel Bank robbery? The Denver & Rio hadn't been much of a triumph, with that mess-up about the safe; but the San Miguel business had gone off as smooth as you'd want, with over ten thousand to split among the five of them. If O.C. wanted to build him up, he shouldn't leave out the San Miguel. . . .

"That's right, you can believe it, he's seen the elephant an' hearn the owl," Hanks went on. "Now,

Butch an' me are gonna whip you shitheads into *shape*! There's gonna be some *organization*!"

Butch looked at Hanks with interest. This was what he'd had in mind, all right, but he hadn't planned on giving O.C. quite such a starring role in the enterprise.

"An' anybody can't cut it'll get his ass rid outta here. Like two fellers I see," he said, scowling ferociously, "that's s'posed t' be out on guard duty right now but ain't! An' I'll tell you what else—"

Hanks stopped as the faces he was addressing turned uniformly slack-jawed and wide-eyed. He pointed his good ear toward the open doorway and heard the sound that had caused this response: a heavy, soft thudding. He had ridden a mount with muffled hoofs often enough to recognize the sound; a bunch of them, for sure.

"All right!" a voice shouted from the darkness. "We got the whole place surrounded!"

Butch twitched. It couldn't be . . .

Hanks scuttled to the window and peered outside. "It's Ray Bledsoe."

. . . but it was.

"Now . . . come on out, *without* your guns and *with* your hands up!" Bledsoe shouted.

"They got us surrounded," Hanks said to Butch. "What'll we do? *Think* of somethin'."

Butch rapidly weighed the value of a number of possible courses of action, then plumped for the best. "Surrender?"

Hanks looked at him sourly, then turned to the doorway and bawled, "Okay, Ray! You got the drop, you call the turn! Git on out, boys, an' drop your hardware in here."

As the grumbling cowboys began filing out, hands high, to be taken and swiftly shackled by the waiting posse, Hanks glumly said to Butch, "For a man that's knowed for quick thinkin', I don't see as you showed any particular streak of it just now. Seems to me you could of—"

"What?" Butch spread his hands. "If your lookouts had done their job, this wouldn't—"

Two deputies entered the saloon and slapped handcuffs on the snarling Hanks. Ray Bledsoe stepped in behind them. "Let's go, boys. We got a long ride tonight. Hello, Butch."

Butch nodded. Hanks, being shoved toward the door by his captors, looked back and called to Bledsoe, "Why aren't you takin' *him* in?"

"No reason to," the sheriff said. "He was in prison when the Lazy Eleven was rustled."

"How'd *you* know that?" Hanks asked, squinting at Bledsoe.

"I was there the day he got out."

Hanks glared at Butch. "What *kinda* deal you make, Butch? You wouldn't say anything before, but I'd kinda like to know right *now*."

"What?" Butch asked.

"To get outta *prison*. This it?" Hanks held up his handcuffed wrists and rattled the chain that linked them. "You lead him here?"

Butch stared at him. It had never occurred to him that he would ever be suspected of letting his pals down—a man's plans might misfire a bit now and then, but no one had ever accused Butch Cassidy of not being straight, except in the matter of breaking some laws now and then. "Lead him?" he said plaintively. "Come *on*, O.C., don't be a damn fool!"

Hanks's voice was a low, harsh growl. "I won't be . . . next time." He grabbed at the door jamb as the deputies thrust him through it and called back, "Next time, I'll *kill* you, Butch!" Then he was gone into the darkness.

Alone in the saloon with Butch, Bledsoe said thoughtfully, "Was I you, I think I'd avoid him when he gets out." He crossed to the plank, poured two fingers of whiskey into a glass and, turning toward Butch, raised it. "Long life."

"Thanks," Butch said bitterly. O.C. had once more got an idea into his skull, and probably nothing short of ventilation was ever going to get it out. Nobody would believe the ridiculous story, of course, but no sensible man wanted O.C. Hanks permanently down on him. Long life, indeed!

Bledsoe finished his drink, found a ragged half-slice of bread on the counter, brushed bits of ash and dust from it, and held it in calloused fingers over the coals of the stove.

"Butch, you ain't been outta prison a week," he said wearily, "an' you come right back here to Brown's Hole." He shook his head. "Get the hell outta here. Go somewheres else. Salt Lake, maybe. San Francisco. What the hell, the Sandwich Islands, even South America."

"What the hell would *I* do in South America?"

"I don't care where you go, or even if you stay—long's you get a job of something, find a way to stay outta trouble."

"I don't *want* a job, Ray," Butch explained, as one reasonable man to another. "That kind of life doesn't suit me."

"Damn it!" Bledsoe said, slopping another measure of whiskey into his glass. "What about your promise to the Governor?"

That was unfair, Butch felt. If it weren't that he'd been so set on keeping that promise that he hadn't let on to O.C. about it for fear of being hoorawed into breaking it, he wouldn't have got O.C. set on killing him. "That was Wyoming," he pointed out.

"And this is Utah, is that it?" He slammed the glass down on the rude bar and glowered at Butch. "At least have the decency to think about me! I don't want to arrest you again!"

"*Okay*," Butch said, cheerful again now that he was

getting a chance to negotiate. "Same deal? I won't do *anything* in this general vicinity. I'll stay out of *your* jurisdiction."

Bledsoe took a pull at the glass and shook his head. "How many places can you promise to stay out of, Butch?"

Butch shrugged. "It's a big country."

"Maybe," the sheriff said heavily. "But there's more law around then ever before, now the place is growin' up, fillin' up. Not old farts like me, waitin' out their pensions, hopin' not to get killed. Young men, full of righteous fire. You won't make deals with *them*."

He finished his drink, gave Butch a somber look, and left.

In the deserted saloon, Butch pondered what Ray Bledsoe had said. The West *was* filling in, the way a plowed field next to a meadow will get choked with weeds. Towns, new rail lines, telegraph and telephone wires spreading out to tangle a man who used to be able to count on his own speed and agility to keep ahead of pursuers, a whole plague of dried-up old-maid schoolteachers . . . and the lawmen, just as Ray had said. Not the easygoing breed like Masterson and Earp, who might be on one side of the badge one day and the other the next, and always ready to treat the fellow they dealt with like a man and brother, but law-and-order fanatics like that Le Fors. . . . He shook his head with a grin. Ace tracker and hard-nosed as he was, Le Fors hadn't been able to take that scatterwitted kid forted up on the mesa. Without saying a word or firing a shot, the kid had made Le Fors deal himself out of the game. Be *something* to have a fellow like that siding you. Provided you could gentle him enough so he'd take a bit in his mouth . . .

Butch sighed and upended an opened bottle on the plank bar into his mouth. Only a swallow, but maybe that was enough. He could sit here and work his way through the remnants of the saloon's stock—the proprietor as well as the customers having been caught up in Bledsoe's net, there'd be no one to complain or demand payment—and wind up in the morning with a splitting head and a mouth like a buffalo wallow. Or he could do the sensible thing and get on back to his cabin, brew up some coffee, and give some intensive thought as to just what the hell he would do next.

Put that way, it was a damned hard decision.

He compromised by tucking a half-full bottle into a coat pocket, and leaving the saloon. Butch's horse was still there, he was relieved to see; Ray must have recognized it as his.

Riding back to the cabin, a thought struck him: What about O.C.'s Emma? With her man away, and hardly anybody left in the area, she would probably be looking for a new protector, and there weren't many candidates besides Butch. Yet what if, visiting O.C. in jail, she got infected with his crazy notion, and came gunning for him. It was hard to say which prospect was less appetizing. Whatever plans he made, they had better include moving on, soon.

At the cabin clearing, the glow of the light from the fire he'd left going was cheering. Butch dismounted, threw the reins over his horse's head, and started to unbuckle the saddle cinch.

He stopped as a horse nickered—close by but invisible in the darkness. He slid his revolver out of its holster and dropped to one knee, keeping his horse between himself and the direction from which the sound of the other animal had come.

After a moment, he moved quietly in a crouch to the nearest tree and then the next, working toward where the sound now came again. Outlined against the sky, he saw the horse—riderless, but saddled and bridled.

Butch looked toward his cabin. In the firelit window he saw a flicker of motion. O.C.'s Emma, waiting to bushwhack him? Someone waiting to settle an old score? Whoever, it was likely to be bad news.

He stalked to the cabin and flattened himself against the wall, then began inching toward the window, his gun held high.

He paused next to the window frame, took a deep breath, and darted his head forward, holding the pistol ready to smash the pane and fire.

Through the murky distortion of the cheap glass, a surprised face was staring back at him.

"What the hell are you *doin'* out there?" it said.

Butch let the held breath out in a long whoosh and slid the revolver back in the holster. It was the kid from Anderson's and the mesa.

CHAPTER SIX

"Nice place," the kid said, cockily tilted back in a chair and looking around the cabin.

Butch, still fuming from the shock of encountering the kid again, added some logs to the fire. "*Yeah*, well, us outlaws live high off the *hog*. What do you want?"

The kid tilted back until the chair was nearly balanced on the two rear legs. Butch had a sudden flickering recollection of himself as a kid and his mother, telling him over and over to stop doing just that.

"I got to thinking about what you said."

"What's that?" Butch said curtly, stirring the fire into life with a crudely fashioned poker.

The kid almost lost his balance, then regained it and settled the chair's front legs on the floor. He stared at the floor planks for a moment, then looked up at Butch. "You know . . . about joining up?"

Butch had not yet calmed down. A man gets worked up for a shootout, he told himself, it's gonna take a *while* before he feels like being sociable and businesslike. And, after hours of cleaning up after O.C. and Emma, he wasn't too glad to have uninvited guests, anyway. Either a man's cabin is the waiting room of the Union Pacific depot or it isn't, was his opinion, and he'd be prepared to bet a considerable sum that his wasn't.

"Seems to me I heard you worked *alone*," he said scornfully.

The kid sprang to his feet, knocking the chair backward. In the dim firelight, he was as tense as a coiled rattler, and spoke with a harsh edge to his voice: "A while ago *you* wanted to join up with *me!*"

"Well, now, I'm not so sure," Butch said mildly, keeping a tight grip on the poker. "You've got a nasty temper—"

The kid's hand drifted toward his gun.

"—but I'm sure you've got your *good* qualities, too." He paused. This wasn't quite the same as taking on someone like Harve or Elza Lay for a job—do it, split the take, and run like hell in different directions. What was on the table now was a partnership. The kid had the hard, driving, reckless quality that Butch lacked; and Butch had the free-ranging imagination the kid didn't have. Together they could make one hell of a unit and pull things off that neither of them could have done alone or with a lesser partner. And that was the rub, Butch felt. Once they came to a deal, there'd be no turning back—he and this kid would be on a trail that might go a long way and wind through some interesting territory before it came to . . . wherever it ended at. He could send the kid on his way right now, or . . .

"Okay," he said.

The kid relaxed and a smile spread on his face. It surprised Butch; it was the first time he'd seen the kid look anything but tough and dangerous, and it made quite a change.

The kid righted the chair and settled into it again. "Seeing as we're partners now, how about some grub? I haven't eaten since this morning."

Butch whittled some bacon off the slab he'd bought at Bridgeport, set it frying on the fire in a battered pan, and went to open a can of beans. "Listen," he said, "I've gotta call you something. What in hell's your name, anyway?"

He dumped the beans in with the sizzling bacon and stirred them together. Not restaurant cooking, but quick and filling. Better than anything O.C.'s Emma had likely been making this last year, anyhow.

"Longabaugh," the kid said after a moment. "Harry Longabaugh."

Butch looked up from his place at the fire. "Longabaugh. *That's* no outlaw's name." He studied the kid. "You don't have an outlaw's face, either. You ought to do something with it."

The kid ran one hand over his face. "Like what?"

"I don't know. Get a nice scar, grow a moustache. Something." The beans were bubbling now. Butch ladled the food onto two tin plates, and carried them to the table. He sat down and shoved one plate to the other side of the table. The kid hitched his chair over and dug into the meal.

After his first mouthful, the kid laid down his spoon and said earnestly, "I *am* growing a moustache."

Butch squinted at him. "Where?"

Longabaugh self-consciously pointed to his upper lip. Butch leaned across the table and was able to make out a faint line of fuzz. "How long you been workin' on that?"

"Not long," Longabaugh said carelessly, as if hoping to suggest that the idea had struck him just before shaving that morning.

"*How* long?" Butch persisted.

Longabaugh's face reddened a little. "What's the difference? It's, uh, slow starting." He glared at Butch. "*Look,* are we gonna rob something or not?!"

"Yeah, we're gonna rob *something*." A slow smile started on Butch's face as he realized what the job would be—what it logically, beautifully *had* to be.

Longabaugh leaned forward excitedly, careless of the fact that the spoon he was holding was dripping beans and bacon onto his fist. "A train?" he said eagerly. "How 'bout a train?"

Butch held up an admonitory hand and shook his head. "You just don't go and rob a *train*. That takes

69

practice. We gotta work together for a while first. Work *up* to it."

"A bank, then."

"No. A casino."

"Okay." Longabaugh licked the beans from his fist and looked at Butch expectantly. Butch grinned. The kid seemed ready for anything. Be interesting to see how hot he was for the proposition after one or two details were spelled out . . .

"That casino," he said. "The one you messed up on last week."

Longabaugh looked at him incredulously. "*I* can't go back there. They'll recognize me."

Butch leaned over and picked a cushion from the floor. It was one of the few damageable items that O.C. and Emma had left intact. He ripped it along a seam, dug out a handful of horsehair, and squinted speculatively at Longabaugh's face. Longabaugh stared back. His expression made it clear that he was wondering what was the use of tying up with a partner if the partner was going to go crazy ten minutes after the deal was set.

Authorities have argued for years over what distinction, if any, there is between tramps and hoboes. Hoboes are said to have a widespread though loose organization and to share a mystic language of signs, which, chalked on fence posts and the like, indicate such dangers as watchdogs, hot-tempered farmers, and alert cops, and such blessings as unguarded chicken coops, farm wives who are free with food, and chances for odd jobs. They are also believed to congregate in otherwise unusable areas on the outskirts of towns, called "jungles," and sit around exchanging lies while eating an indescribable stew known as mulligan from tin cans. Hoboes look down on tramps, who are merely loners wandering across the country in search of work, but to the outsider there is little or no difference.

The bent figure in worn, greasy clothes and a tattered coat leaning into the chill wind as it trudged through the high grass outside Steamboat Springs might have been that of either a hobo or a tramp. It was drab and discouraged, which would have given weight to the tramp opinion; but the beard and moustache—stiff and spiky as horsehair—smacked more of the hobo, tramps tending to shave when they can. Whichever he might be, a farmer or rancher seeing him would automatically put himself in easy reach of a shotgun or pitchfork.

Longabaugh scratched at the beard and cursed. The glue that held the horsehair to his face was drawing up the skin of his chin and upper lip, and itched like hell. The glue also stank. He had never known glue was made from what was left after you boiled horses' hides and hoofs for a long time, but it was a fact he would never now forget.

A man that rode with the Daltons or the James boys didn't get into this kind of situation, he reflected gloomily. With fellows like that, you go in, take what you want, and ride out. But no, Harry Longabaugh had to sign articles with a guy with *imagination*, a man that knew how to *plan*. So here he was, dressed in lousy old rags that looked as though they'd been stolen off a couple of scarecrows—which they had: the first Longabaugh-Cassidy exploits had been a daring raid on a couple of cornfields, to Longabaugh's strongly expressed disgust—plodding through the fields. *And* stinking of glue.

The buildings at the edge of town were in sight now, and he stopped and squinted at them. Now there was one thing old Butch *hadn't* thought out. A crummy tramp might not attract much attention, fine. But a tramp smelling strongly of glue? Someone like that, folks get to wondering things, like just *what* is glued to *what* and why? Those fake-looking whiskers, maybe . . . ?

71

Longabaugh did not know that his worries about the distinctive odor of the glue were within a few seconds of being taken care of. It would have made him not one bit happier if he *had* known.

He stopped: something had moved in the high grass in front of him. A rattler? Not likely right here, they liked the rocky places better . . .

"Hell!"

Longabaugh scrabbled under the bulky coat for his pistol and stumbled as he took a backward step. Like most men who have put in time as cowhands, he feared and hated skunks; he had known men poisoned nearly fatally by skunk bites received while they slept in the open, and was firmly convinced that they carried hydrophobia, and should be destroyed on sight.

The unfamiliar coat slowed his draw. The startled skunk was under no such disadvantage, and fired a split second before Longabaugh's wild shot, then disappeared into the grass.

Whooping and cursing, Longabaugh staggered in erratic circles. Shooting off the rest of his cartridges into the grass in the general direction of the vanished skunk did little to relieve his feelings.

The skunk's weapon had, luckily, not taken him in the eyes but struck the midsection of his coat. The stench caught in his throat and made his eyes water. He scrubbed at the spot with handfuls of grass for a few minutes, but gave up. He now had skunk-stink on his hands as well as the rest of him, and the horrible odor had not abated at all.

He glared toward the town and muttered one short word that carried all the force and venom of the filthiest invective a hardened muleskinner could have devised:

"*Plans!*"

CHAPTER SEVEN

Butch leaned against the bar at Anderson's casino and looked with appreciative interest at one of his favorite sights: money. Crumpled bills, new bills, battered coins, bright coins . . . hundreds of dollars were being handed over by the dealers and dropped into the box the big man in the dark suit was carrying around the room. Butch recognized him as Anderson's balcony rifleman and the part-time deputy who had handed his badge back to Le Fors when the posse turned back. Another man, carrying a shotgun and peering constantly around, followed him.

Wonder if those fellows ever get notions? Butch speculated. Just make the rounds as usual, then go on upstairs to the counting room, pass on by and out the back door, and keep going? Easy as kiss your hand.

He hoped the guards stayed honest for at least—he checked the banjo clock on the wall—another half-hour. Ten past six would be about the right time. Harry should be striking town about now, and everything else was set up.

Only half the gaming tables were in operation, and these were sparsely patronized, as was the bar. The orchestra, unmindful of the thin crowd, was working away at "Aura Lee." Good. Nice and quiet, the way he'd planned on.

Two workmen were struggling to hoist a bent and battered chandelier, hung with mismatched crystals— evidently Anderson had filled in the damage with what he could find locally. Butch grinned as he noted that the chandelier was now supported by a chain, not a rope. He never had asked Harry if those shots had been lucky or deliberate. No point to it; he'd be bound to claim it was a display of coolness and skill under fire.

He drummed his fingers on the bar and checked the clock again. It was about time for Harry to show up, and getting to be past time. He went to the saloon's door and looked out.

Slouched against the wall near the far edge of the building was a dispirited derelict he had no difficulty in recognizing as his partner. For some reason, passersby were giving him a wide berth; even dogs and horses kept well away from him. And why the hell hadn't he joined Butch inside as he'd been told to?

Butch approached Longabaugh frowning. "What are you doing out—"

He slowed, stopped, and sniffed.

Longabaugh glared at him. "*Terrific* idea of yours, me coming in through the fields."

Butch bit hard in the inside of his cheek. It would not do to laugh.

"You think it's funny?" Longabaugh said hotly.

"*No*," Butch said in as soothing a tone as he could manage. A man ought to be honest with his partner, but there are situations that call for an unabashed lie.

" 'No one'll ever look at a tramp,' " Longabaugh said bitterly. "Isn't that what you said?" He jerked his head toward a rider who, though some distance past them, was peering over his shoulder in fascination. He levered himself away from the wall. "Let's get outta here. Maybe we can plan something that don't call for quite so much play-actin'."

Butch grabbed his arm. "Are you *kidding*? This is the perfect time—you oughtta see all the money they're putting in that strongbox. That counting room has got to be loaded!"

"I'm not going in there," Longabaugh said.

"Hey, you really don't smell that bad, Harry," Butch said earnestly. "It's just, uh, the first whiff. After that you kinda get used to it. Really. I mean, cowhands, fellows that work in stables an' so on, they're not any rosebuds either, and they come here regular. You'll fit right in. Now, come on."

Longabaugh glared hard at Butch, but finally shoved past him and entered the saloon. Butch let out the deep breath he had been holding and followed his partner in.

It was close to a dozen years since Butch had looked into a Bible, and then mainly because there'd been some pretty racy stuff once you could figure out the old-time language it was in, but he was vividly reminded of the effect the approach of Moses had had on the Red Sea. Anderson's clientele moved quickly, one or two in their haste overturning a chair, to leave Longabaugh a clear and wide path to the bar. The bartender, stationed at the far end, made two steps toward him, then four back.

"I thought you said it wasn't so bad!" Longabaugh muttered.

"Well, I lied," Butch said reasonably. He went on hastily, to forestall the furious retort Longabaugh was obviously about to make: "I've made all the arrangements. You're gonna love it."

"What arrangements?" Longabaugh asked, looking wistfully at the array of bottles behind the bar.

"Them." Butch jerked a thumb toward the end of the bar. Two girls—one the pockmarked doxy Butch had been offered on his previous visit to Anderson's, the other considerably prettier and more robust—stood there, out of range of Longabaugh's aura, flashing inviting smiles that appeared to be maintained with some difficulty.

"Ruby and Annie," Butch said. "Ruby's the one in the red dress. She's really a swell kid."

"Tough, too," Longabaugh said morosely, "to of got over a case of the smallpox like that. Way you're talking, Butch, I got a feeling Ruby's mine, right?"

"Well . . ." Butch looked uneasy. "After all, it's not as if—"

"Yah, that's the *good* side of it," Longabaugh said. "Mighty interestin' *plan* when one of the great things *about* it is you get set up with a woman an' don't get to go to bed with her. Not many fellows I heard of could come up with plans like that."

Butch ignored this comment and made for the girls. Longabaugh, still grumbling, followed him. Three patrons who had been edging toward Annie and Ruby backed off hurriedly, but the girls stood their ground. Butch's promises had been generous, and, in any case, they had their professional pride.

"Well," Butch said heartily, "my friend's here now, so we can all get on upstairs and inspect those rooms everyone speaks so high of."

He looked over at the collector and the man guarding him with the shotgun. One more table to go; then they would head on upstairs and to the counting room, as it had cost him a gold eagle to find out from the saloon's swamper. That would put them in the right place at the right time. . . .

The buxom Annie took Butch's arm with a radiant smile and moved him quickly toward the stairs, not so much in anticipation of delights to come, he estimated, as to put some distance between them and Longabaugh and Ruby.

Ruby, breathing shallowly, said to Longabaugh, "Listen, I better tell you I'm a fresh-air fiend, see? I mean, windows wide open and all, okay?"

"Pretty chilly now," Longabaugh said. "Don't you get goose bumps?"

"There's worse things than goose bumps," she said, keeping as far from him as the width of the staircase permitted.

"We ever been together before, you and me?" Annie asked Butch. "You look familiar."

"I got kind of an average face," Butch said with a shrug. "Everything about me is kind of average, in fact."

Annie gave him an appraising glance and raised one eyebrow. "That's too bad."

"Where you boys come from?" Ruby asked, her tone indicating no particular interest in the answer.

"Canada," Longabaugh said, as Butch had directed. Any oddities in their behavior, he had suggested, might be accounted for by their being foreigners. Thought of *everything*, Butch did, Longabaugh reflected. Trouble was, sometimes what he'd thought of didn't work out the way it was supposed to.

Ruby looked him over and nodded. "You look Canadian."

As Longabaugh tried to work out whether he should feel insulted on behalf of his temporarily adopted country, Annie stopped a few feet ahead of them in the upstairs corridor, reached between her ample breasts, and withdrew a key.

Butch glanced back to the head of the stairs. Good—the two guards were just coming up, carrying the money box.

"This is us, honey," Annie said, unlocking and opening a door. Butch leaned forward past her and looked around the room as the guards passed the foursome. They stopped at a door halfway down the hall and knocked.

Butch turned and pointed to the door opposite to the one the guards were waiting at. "What's next door?"

"That's the Red Room," Annie said. "But you don't get in *there* for ten bucks."

"Never mind the cost," Butch said grandly. "I like the sound of that . . . the Red Room. What's red about it?"

"Everything," Annie said. She nodded to her co-worker. "Ruby, you use this one. Big Spender wants the Red Room."

"Okay," Ruby said. "Got two windows, anyways."

Longabaugh made no move to enter the room immediately, and Ruby did not urge him. As Annie, now at the entrance to the Red Room, explored her décolletage for another key, Butch tensed at the sound of a lock opening and a bolt being thrown from inside the room opposite.

The door opened and the money-laden guards stepped inside. Butch gave a frantic wave to Longabaugh. Both men grabbed their women and burst through the closing door after the guards, drawing their pistols as they slammed it behind them.

"Say, what in the hell are you . . ." a disheveled and indignant Annie started to complain, then stopped. Two armed men bursting into the counting room, and she had to *ask* what they were doing? She hastily stuffed the Red Room key back inside her dress. If that got stolen, along with whatever these fellows were planning to rob Anderson of, she'd be the one who'd have to pay for having a duplicate cut. Ruby had not bothered to protest. Being used as a battering ram and having a gun waved under her nose weren't especially worse than lots of things that happened to her in the course of business.

The guard with the shotgun was still using one hand to help hold the money box; he calculated quickly the chances of aiming and shooting his weapon single-handed in the face of two revolvers, and dropped the idea. The third man in the room, a slightly built fellow wearing a green celluloid eyeshade, looked up at them.

"We'll split with you!" Butch said hurriedly, waving his pistol to cover each of the men in turn.

Longabaugh started. "Split?" he cried plaintively.

"Shut *up*, I'm doin' this," Butch muttered. To the

78

guards and the bookkeeper he said impressively, "I'm
. . . Butch Cassidy."

They did not exactly cower, or gasp in dismay; in
cold fact, they did nothing but continue to goggle at
him. He might as well, he thought, have announced
himself as Arnold Bozeman or J. Davenport Hostetter.
Fellows in a tough town like this *ought* to have heard
of the Denver & Rio Grande robbery and the Denver
First National if they took any interest in what was
going on.

"*That's* right," he said with forced heartiness. "And
this—" he waved his left hand at Longabaugh "—is
Harry . . . the, uh . . . Skunk."

Longabaugh gave him a dangerous look.

"Hey," Ruby said, showing some animation, "I've
hearda *you.*"

Both Butch and Longabaugh looked at her sharply,
wondering who, or what, she could be thinking of.
Billy the *Kid?* Some talking animal in a children's
book? Or *was* there a hardcase of that name they
didn't know about, and if so, how had he earned it?

The shotgun guard—his weapon prudently laid
aside—was puzzling over a problem of more urgency.
"*Why* do you want to split with us?" Bandits, in his
experience, did not declare dividends to the victims.

Butch said smoothly, "Because you seem like nice
folks and I don't want to kill you." He nodded toward
the glowering Harry the Skunk. "Even though *he*
would. Look at him." The three men and two women
did so, and, inwardly or outwardly, shuddered. Longabaugh's lips were twisted in a snarl and his glance was
bright with dislike, seemingly directed as much at his
partner as at any of them. The whiskers alone were
enough to mark him as a man lost to normal stan-
dards.

Butch continued in awed tones. "He's an *animal.* He
hasn't got any feelings at all." This did not strike his
hearers as entirely accurate, as Longabaugh's face was

all too expressive of barely contained rage, but the point was made. "Look," Butch went on ingratiatingly, "what d'you guys make? Eighteen, twenty bucks a week?"

The bookkeeper stiffened in his seat. "Twenty-*two*."

"We split this, you'll be in clover for the next ten *years*! And the best part is, nobody'll suspect *you*. They'll *want* to believe I did it . . . because I'm Butch Cassidy, the outlaw—"

"An' he's Harry the Skunk," Ruby put in brightly. She was proud of being the only person in the room who had heard of the notorious Harry . . . someplace, though right now she couldn't remember just where. But she knew she must have come across it: the name seemed so *right* for him, somehow. . . .

"Now," Butch said, "open the safe."

The guards looked at each other hesitantly, then at the bookkeeper. The bookkeeper looked back at them.

"*Look*," Butch urged. "I can't guarantee he won't *kill* you if you don't open it fast."

The guards and the bookkeeper risked a glance at the notorious Skunk. He was clearly on the point of a murderous explosion.

"I can't hold him back much longer," Butch pleaded.

The former deputy sighed. Marshal Le Fors was down on him, and this afternoon's work was not going to put him ace high with Anderson, for sure. Might be about time to light out for Tombstone or some place quiet like that, since employment opportunities were likely to be pretty slim for him in Steamboat Springs from here on. "Open it, Earl," he told the bookkeeper sadly.

"Don't you worry," Butch said. "I'll take all the blame—and so will he." He nodded toward his associate, then added, "We'll have to knock you out to make it look good."

"Knock us *out*?" the ex-deputy repeated. Whichever way you went with these two, it didn't seem that a man could come out of it anywhere near as healthy as he'd gone in.

"So it won't look like we're *in* on it, stupid!" his partner growled.

The ex-dupty nodded. True enough, better a lump on the skull than the chance of Anderson suspecting something wasn't straight. Anderson carried a powerful lot of weight in town, and a fellow he thought wasn't on the up-and-up stood a pretty good chance of being simply *up*, so to speak, and twisting slowly, slowly in the wind.

The bookkeeper crouched in front of the black iron safe, twirled the knob, swung the handle, and pulled the door open. As Longabaugh approached, he moved quickly away. Longabaugh reached inside and began pulling out rubber-banded stacks of bills and neatly tagged coin sacks and stuffing them into his capacious coat pockets.

"Where do you want us to leave your half?" Butch said.

"How we gonna divide this up?" Annie asked, speaking for the first time since just after she had been thrust into the room. The business with the guns and the safe was all very well for fellows like this Cassidy and his stripy friend, but she was acutely aware that she was losing time, and therefore money. And with the knock-out stuff, and the foofaraw with Anderson there'd be afterward, it'd likely be eight or later before she would be back in business. Annie disliked the idea of even a partial unpaid holiday.

The guards and the bookkeeper were taken aback. They had so far considered themselves the principals in this affair, with the women as onlookers only. "I hadn't . . ." the bookkeeper began, then caught Annie's cold glance. "I suppose pro-rata shares, based on—"

"Nix," Annie said, shaking her head firmly. "No poor rates or that for us, I'll tell you right now. An even split five ways, and that's it. Once we go in for this, everybody's got everybody else by the short and curlies, so nobody better be unhappy about it. Same risk, same share, and nobody gets ideas about spilling the beans to Anderson."

"Fair enough," Butch said. "You gentlemen agree?" He waved the barrel of his pistol amiably at them, and, reluctantly, each of the three men nodded. "Settled, then. Now, about where we leave it . . ."

"You heading south?" the shotgun guard asked.

Butch nodded.

"Well . . ." The guard thought. "'Bout half a mile out there's a fork that goes toward Milner, see? You take that about two miles to the Yampa cutoff. Big sycamores right there. Two of 'em. The one on the *right's* got a big hollow in it, an'—"

Butch cut him off impatiently. "It'll be under the mattress of the bed across the hall."

"Accourse, that's a good place, *too*," the guard agreed hastily. He started to back away as Butch approached him, then stood his ground resignedly with eyes closed. Butch wrapped a glove around his gun butt, and swung it against the side of the man's head with firm precision; the guard slumped to the floor.

"I could *pretend* like I was—" the ex-deputy said, but Butch interrupted with another blow of the revolver's butt, and he joined the other guard in untidy repose.

"You wanna be found on the floor with them or at your desk?" Butch asked the bookkeeper.

"At the desk," the bookkeeper said. "Not so far to fall." Butch honored the request and left him face down in a pile of papers.

Longabaugh had paid no attention to Butch's anesthetic treatments, and was now loaded to capacity with a substantial portion of the safe's contents. He

82

stood up and motioned Butch toward the safe to carry on the good work.

Ruby gave him a crooked grin. "Okay, Harry, me next," she said, tilting her head back and offering her chin.

"Hey!" Annie said.

Ruby turned to her. "Whaddya think, we can just sit here and say we was too scared to holler or something for half an hour after they left? You see Anderson buying that? Say, he'd wear us down till we could go under a door without mussing our hair, you can bet, if he smelled any funny business about this." She looked again at Longabaugh. "So clip me, Harry, an' get it over with, huh?"

Longabaugh nodded and stepped forward, then stopped and turned to where Butch was harvesting the safe. "I never hit a woman, Butch," he said plaintively.

"*Don't* hit her, then," Butch said, stuffing a bundle of bills into his top outside pocket. "We'll just take her *along*. Nice having a woman on the trail with us. Maybe you'll even fall in love and marry her."

Longabaugh sighed, shrugged, and brought a looping right from behind his waist to the point of Ruby's jaw. Her eyes crossed and turned up, her knees buckled, and she fell backward into the arms of Annie, who lowered her to lie limply across a chair.

Butch had by now stuffed his clothing with money, including a couple of sheaves of bills protruding from his boottops. He rose and faced Annie. "You want me to do you—I mean," he said hastily as she gave a snort of laughter, "you know . . ." He flourished his fist. "Not but that . . . well . . ."

She shook her head. "He hits, *you* field." She wrinkled her nose. "I gotta wear this dress for work later, and if Harry the Skunk here was to catch me so's I wouldn't fall hard, no offense, but it'd be a week's airing before I could use it again."

Longabaugh had to admit the justice of her comment; but all the same, his punch to her jaw was not pulled quite so much as the one that had decked Ruby.

"What the *hell* are you doin'?!" Longabaugh whispered a few moments later as Butch paused by the door opposite the counting room. "We got to get outta here!"

"I'm leaving the money," Butch answered. "Their half." He brought a key out of a shirt pocket and unlocked the door.

Longabaugh's eyes bulged, and only the need for silence kept him from screaming like a wounded panther. "But you just *said* that, to . . ." He gritted his teeth.

Butch raised his eyebrows. "This is the first those folks ever heard of Butch Cassidy," he pointed out. "You wouldn't want me to get a bad name, would you?" He stepped into the room, and Longabaugh closed his eyes, his lips moving in what might have been silent prayer, or the reverse, as he heard the crackling sounds of money being inserted under the mattress. Bad name! he thought. You want bad names, Mister Cassidy, I got a *load* of 'em for you right now!

His eyes snapped open and he looked thoughtfully at the door. Last time he'd seen the key to it, Annie had been stuffing it back down the front of her dress. Just when had Butch retrieved it? Oh, yeah . . . when he'd caught her after the knockout punch. And what would you want to bet, Longabaugh asked himself, that he hadn't taken his damn *time* about hunting it out, too!

CHAPTER EIGHT

A flung handful of snowflakes stung their faces and clouded their vision for a few seconds, then was gone. The sandstone strata of the canyon country, which, under full sunlight would dazzle and glare, lay around them as sullenly dull as old iron under the lead-gray sky. They moved through pulsing, intermittent clouds of steamlike condensed moisture exhaled by their laboring horses.

Butch and Longabaugh, slouched inside their heavy coats against the autumn cold, let the horses carry them along. They had been on the trail for days, long enough to be sure that there was no hot pursuit as a result of their looting Anderson's casino. They would be on the way for days more; there was no place on their route worth stopping at any time soon, unless you counted Glenwood Springs, where the Roaring Fork met the Colorado, and that was too well connected with civilization, what with telegraph and the D&RG line, to be comfortable for travelers who didn't care to answer any questions about what they might have been up to in Steamboat Springs.

"You ever been to Telluride?" Butch said, some half an hour after the last exchange of conversation between them.

"I don't think so," Longabaugh answered. "Where's it at? Aside from bein' where we're headed for, which is some distance I don't know in some direction I hope you're sure of."

"San Miguel County, sort of between Ophir and Saw Pit," Butch said proudly. "You'd remember it if you'd been there. It's *terrific*. Lotta big outlaws hole up there for the winter. Great hotels . . . fancy restaurants . . . best-looking women you ever saw."

Longabaugh ignored this catalogue of the enticements of Telluride, and said abruptly, "You figure they'll put out a Wanted poster on us now?"

Butch considered this. "Maybe. Why?"

Longabaugh peered abashedly at him from under his hat brim. "I never had one," he said. "Kind of makes you *somebody*, you know?"

Butch nodded. The only Wanted notice he'd ever seen posted for himself had his name spelled as "Cassady," and the picture seemed to have been printed from an engraving plate made of bread, but there was no denying that it gave a man a feeling of having arrived. "Well," he said after a moment, "if you want your name on a poster, it oughta be something better than Harry Longabaugh. That stinks."

"I know," Longabaugh said tiredly. "But I'm not much at thinking up names."

Butch pondered as the horses stolidly picked their way along the stony path. "Let's see . . . Long-a-baugh . . . *Longa*baugh . . . Longa*baugh* . . ." The rhythm of his horse's hoofbeats echoed the meter of the name as he spoke it but did not inspire any ideas.

"I called myself Harry Alonzo for a while," Longabaugh reminisced.

Butch looked at him curiously. "Alonzo? What for?"

" 'S my middle name."

Butch studied his horse's laid-back ears for a moment, then called to his companion. "I'd keep that a secret. You remember that O.C. Hanks I was talkin' about?"

"Yeah. What about him? Come to names, I don't think O.C.'s so hot."

"Better than what the *C* stands for, anyhow," Butch

said. "Found it out one time when he was dead drunk, which he was when he could get, but this was deader than usual, if you take my meaning."

"Claude? Chauncy? Somethin' that bad?"

"*Camilla,*" Butch said in a voice that might have issued from a tomb.

Longabaugh stared at him, then threw his head back and crowed. "Highty-tighty, Lord almighty, Camilla! Big old rustler, bad man and all-around hardcase, and he's named Camilla! Why, Alonzo an' Longabaugh *together* ain't nothing to that!" He broke off and stared at Butch. "Hey . . . if the *C*'s Camilla, what's the *O* stand for?"

Butch shook his head. "Drunk, dead drunk, or hung over, he *never* told that. If he could spill Camilla an' not mind so much, except for huntin' me up later and tellin' me he'd geld me with a rusty saw, I so much as let on to anyone about that, seems to me that *O* must be pretty strong medicine."

Half an hour later the terrain had leveled off enough so that their horses could proceed at a canter; this advantage was balanced by increasingly spiteful spats of snow. Butch was still working through possible names for his partner.

"Cherokee Charlie," he mused. "Buck Barton . . . Johnny Ringo . . ."

That last had a nice sound to it, but he shook his head. "Already taken. Lucky Wilson . . ." He looked toward Longabaugh, who grimaced.

"Well, then," Butch said, nettled, "will you *help*? I need a little inspiration here. Haven't you ever done anything interesting?"

"I was in jail once," Longabaugh said, deciding that it would be mean-spirited to ask if robbing Anderson's casino twice, standing off the redoubtable Joe Le Fors, trying conclusions with a skunk, and decking two hookers didn't *some* way qualify as interesting.

"Where?"

"Sundance, Wyoming. Sort of halfway between the Devil's Tower and Beulah, but some south of both. Wasn't for anything much, but . . ."

He stopped, seeing that Butch was deep in creative thought.

"Kid Sundance," Butch said, then shook his head. "No, it doesn't quite have . . ." He stopped, and his face lit up. "The Sundance Kid."

Longabaugh straightened in his saddle and looked at his partner. Butch looked back. "I *like* that," Longabaugh said.

"So do I," Butch said. "In fact, I like it so much *I* want it. You can be Butch Cassidy."

Longabaugh shook his head. "Nope, it's mine. I was in jail there, not you, so I got it." The same slow, rare smile that he had displayed when Butch had agreed that they should join forces spread over his face. "The Sundance Kid."

He squared his shoulders and faced ahead into the gray sky. A squire of the Round Table, rising after the touch of King Arthur's sword on his shoulder, and realizing that he was henceforth Sir Whatever-it-was, might have worn the same expression.

CHAPTER NINE

Butch Cassidy and the Sundance Kid, as befits gentlemen outlaws when in funds, left their horses in the care of the stable hand in Telluride's largest livery establishment. As they walked through the cavernous stable toward the street, Butch's face glowed with anticipation. Gas and electric lights flared in the street outside the open stable door, softened and made more inviting by a veil of falling snow. Not far off a string orchestra was playing "Clementine," joined in the chorus by a woman singer. Butch liked the sound of her voice. Maybe she'd be as pretty as Annie . . . and, if not, there'd be plenty others to choose from.

"Wait'll you see, Sundance," he said eagerly. "There's nothing like it. It's Telluride!"

"Uh-huh." Sundance was not prepared to be impressed in advance of sampling whatever Telluride might have to offer. He had never seen the fun in getting all worked up over something that might turn out differently from what you expected. Butch, now, was strong on hope and imagination and such, which made him good—sometimes—at planning, but let him in for lots of disappointments, and Sundance, thinking about it, decided he didn't care for disappointments one bit. Butch could bounce back after them, but they just made Sundance killing mad.

As they were about to step out into the snowy street, they stopped and turned at the sound of a muffled sneeze.

From the gloom beside the doorway, a hoarse voice said, "Get 'em up!"

"Telluride. I love it already," Sundance muttered to Butch. They raised their hands above their heads.

They could now see a shadowy figure facing them, holding a gun aimed at them. It motioned with this for them to step forward.

Closer to the holdup man, they relaxed somewhat. Allowing for the shapeless hat he wore, he could not be much taller than five and a half feet, and the gun he pointed at them was shaking, requiring the use of his left arm to steady it. The muffler he wore over the lower part of his face concealed his expression, but they suspected it was not particularly intimidating.

Poor bastard's either scared stiff or froze, Butch concluded. No trouble in him, 'spite of that hogleg he's waving.

I could chop that out of his hand and put a slug through his brisket before he'd have time to spit, Sundance thought.

"G-gimme ever'thing you got," the holdup man quavered.

Butch tapped his chest. "It's inside here."

The holdup man stepped forward, pressed the gun into Butch's ribs and tried to unbutton the heavy topcoat with his left hand. He was wearing no gloves and Butch could see that his fingers were pale—probably on the edge of frostbite. They clawed at the top button without effect.

"Need some help?" Sundance said.

The holdup man ignored the offer and said desperately to Butch, "J-just st-stand still! Quit m-movin'." His breath came hoarsely, and his teeth chattered when he was not speaking. Scared *and* frozen, Butch decided.

"I *am* standing still," Butch pointed out. "*You're* what's movin'."

The holdup man scrabbled at the button, and gave

a faint moan of hopelessness. The disguising muffler slipped from his face. Butch and Sundance were startled to see that he was old—well past sixty. He reached up to adjust the muffler, but succeeded only in unwinding it further. For an instant, he seemed to be juggling the muffler and his gun; then the gun dropped into the snow at his feet.

"Lordy . . ." the old man wailed, and stooped over, running his hands through the snow.

"This one of the big outlaws that hangs out here?" Sundance asked Butch sardonically.

Butch ignored him, bent over, and fished the gun from the snow. The old man straightened and looked at it wistfully. "What are you doing out here," Butch said sternly, "trying to rob innocent people?"

The old man hung his head. "I need five hundred dollars."

"Five *hundred*," Butch said thoughtfully.

"Whatever y-you can sp-spare, sir," the old man said quickly. "I'll get the r-rest from the n-next guy."

"The next guy'll probably *kill* you!" Sundance said. The conversation was beginning to make him uneasy. When a man has the drop on you and you get his gun away from him, there are a couple of things you can do. You can boot his butt away from there, fast, or you can give him a more permanent kind of discouragement. But what you don't do is, you don't go chatting with him about his money troubles.

"What do you need that much for?" Butch continued. Sundance closed his eyes and shook his head.

"We've got a little r-ranch outsida town—"

"You and your wife?"

"My mother."

Sundance looked sharply at Butch, then rolled his eyes. That eager interest on his partner's face was a bad sign.

"W-we had a b-bad year," the old man went on, blowing on his stiffened fingers. "The crops failed an'

91

the cow died an' we c-can't pay off the bank an' he's c-comin' in the *mornin'* to c-c'lect."

"Now tell us about your starving dog," Sundance said bitterly.

"Shut up, Sundance," Butch said absently, still studying the despairing, worn face before him.

The old man's lips quivered and a tear started in the corner of each eye. He sniffed and rubbed his eyes with his coat sleeve.

Butch sighed, opened the top button of his coat, and reached inside. He withdrew a sheaf of bills and began counting them off, squinting to make sure of the denominations in the dim light.

"What are you *doing*?" Sundance said, but with no real inquiry in his voice. It was all too damned *clear* what the brains of the outfit was up to.

"I'm giving him five hundred dollars." Butch pressed the bills into the old man's hand, stuffing the rest of the sheaf—considerably slimmer, Sundance noted bitterly—back inside his coat.

The old man looked blankly at the bills in his hand, then up at Butch. "*All* of it?"

"That's right," Butch said. "Now, you just make sure you tell everybody that—" he straightened to stand a little taller "—Butch Cassidy gave it to you."

"Butch . . . Cassidy," the old man said blankly.

"You don't know who I am?" Butch said, stung. Sundance grinned.

"No, I'm s-sorry, sir, I don't." The old man shook his head.

"I'm a fairly well-known outlaw," Butch said severely.

The old man nodded, taking this in. "Yes, sir." He threw a nervous glance at Butch and licked his lips. If his strange benefactor got upset about not being known, the old man wondered, who was to say he wouldn't change his mind and take the money back? It would be no more peculiar than giving it to him in the first place. Had these two maybe escaped from the lunatic asylum in Denver? News took a while to get to Telluride, especially once the snow set in. . . .

"Maybe not so well known around here as other places," Butch conceded. "Wyoming, for instance. Parts of Utah."

"I'll b-bet you're *very* well known in those places," the old man said quickly, eager to please. "*Famous*, even. In fact, I b-b'lieve I *have* heard of you, Mister . . ."

"Cassidy," Butch said coldly.

"Cassidy!" The old man snapped his numbed fingers. "*That's* right—Dutch Cassidy. I'll be sure an' let ever'body kn-know it was you give me this money, sir. . . ."

As he spoke, he had been backing off; now, at the doorway, he raised his hat, stuffed the money inside his coat, and scuttled off into the falling snow.

"This is a high-rolling town, all right," Sundance said. "We ain't had so much as a drink, or give a young lady the glad eye, or tried our luck against the house, an' we're already down five hundred bucks. Do you expect we can make it as far as the nearest saloon an' still have some funds left for some of them diversions?"

"Now, Sundance," Butch said mildly. "I know what you're thinking."

They stepped through the stable door and into the street. Sundance studied Butch closely. "Funny," he said. "You ain't turning pale or reaching for your gun or falling down in a fit, and you'd be doin' *some* of them things if you was reading my mind at all clear."

"What you're not doing is thinking ahead," Butch said. "All you see is me handing five hundred over to that old geezer—"

"That does occupy my thoughts considerable, yes." Sundance looked at Butch curiously. Another Cassidy plan coming across the horizon like a prairie fire?

"But then he's gonna hand it over to someone *else*, right . . . ?"

The snowfall dimmed the outlines of the cabin and outbuildings, giving the scene the picturesque look of an Old Homestead in a Currier & Ives engraving. But his practiced eye could tell, even from where he and Sundance waited on their horses in a stand of trees some distance off, that the place was in sad disrepair. An outbuilding was about to collapse; several fences already had; the cabin was swaybacked with a definite lean to the left; and the thin trickle of smoke from the stone chimney testified that on this ranch wood had to be hoarded as strictly as cash, to be used stick by stick, no matter how bitter the weather. The only element of the scene that spoke of care or prosperity was the sleek horse tied to a post outside the cabin; and it was snorting and stamping impatiently, almost as if it meant to make clear that it had no connection with this place and would like to be away from it as quickly as possible.

Butch shook his head. It was back-breaking work to keep a spread in shape, no doubt about it. He hadn't been all that fond of work back at the home place near Circleville, but he'd known it had to be done—and Maximilian Parker, even with a home-grown work force of thirteen kids, had damned well seen to it that his first son had done more than his share of it. It was a shame to see a ranch fall to rack and ruin . . . maybe he and Sundance could put in a little time here, help these folks with some chores and rebuilding. He glanced at the morose Sundance seated next to him, huddled inside his fur collar and turned-down hat brim. No, that wasn't in the cards. Sundance would stand a lot of surprises, but not being turned into a hired man. Anyhow, what was the point of being an outlaw if you were going to drop it for regular work?

Sundance blew on his hands, then stuffed them back

inside his gloves. "I don't know about you," he said, "but I'm freezing my ass off. This isn't worth it."

"I'm telling you," Butch said patiently, "that five hundred bucks will buy us a lot of goodwill around these parts. You saw that look on that old man's face. He looked at me like I was . . . some kind of hero."

Sundance had read the old man's expression more accurately—some kind of loony was more like it—and gave Butch a disgusted look. "That's what you want to be? A hero?"

Butch was surprised. "Haven't you ever wanted to be a hero, have little kids look up to you?"

Sundance leaned over and spat into the snow.

"When I was a kid *my* hero was an outlaw," Butch continued dreamily. "Mike Cassidy. I even took his name. He *was* the best, Sundance. Never saw anybody like him on a horse. Fastest on the draw—"

Sundance decided it was time to have some fun on his own. "I could beat him," he said solemnly.

"What?" Butch looked at him with indignation. "You never even *saw* him!"

"I could beat him," Sundance repeated.

"You think you're that good, huh?"

Sundance nodded. Butch was straight up in the saddle, glaring at him, and he had to work to keep a straight face.

"I suppose," Butch said with scorn, "you could beat Doc Holliday, too."

"I'd blow his damn head off," Sundance stated. "Whoever he is."

Butch snorted. No wonder people weren't familiar with the name of Butch Cassidy, if even a fellow in the trade didn't know about one of the really great ones. It sometimes seemed that most folks couldn't keep hold of anything that had happened before last Thursday; probably ask anybody about the Daltons, even, and they'd think you meant the new saddlemaker and his family, only their name's Darcy, was that who you meant?

"*Was*," he said, aiming for a crushing tone. "He's dead."

Sundance turned a face of complete innocence toward him. "I thought you said he was *good*."

Speechless, Butch glared at him, then turned away. He stiffened and made an urgent gesture. Sundance followed it and saw coming from the cabin a burly man in a fur coat. The man's head was bent in concentration as he counted through a sheaf of bills he held in his hands. The would-be holdup man of the previous night followed him out and stood looking silently as the burly man stuffed the bills in his pocket, mounted his horse, and rode off. Neither the old rancher or the rider waved or called any farewells.

"Some disappointed he didn't get to foreclose," Butch observed. "Bankers get a taste for that, I hear."

"Foreclose on that place," Sundance said, "an' you'd wish you could give it back in about six months. I don't know that you done that old man that much of a favor."

"It was what he had his heart set on," Butch answered. "That's what counts. Now, let's get on with it."

As they had planned, they came upon the banker about a quarter of a mile down the trail. Moving silently in from each side out of the trees, they were not noticed until the man looked up to find himself flanked by two riders, nothing visible of their faces except the tips of their noses between their pulled-up mufflers and lowered hat brims.

The one on his left nodded slowly in greeting but said nothing. The banker looked quickly toward the other, who did not even nod but sat his horse with a casual stolidity.

The banker quickly considered a number of things he might do or say under these unnerving circumstances. None of them seemed at all worthwhile. A sprightly comment about the weather as a conversational opening would make no sense. And anything like trying to dodge away would be—

"Dangerous," the one on his left said in a sepulchral tone, uncannily carrying on the banker's train of thought. "Out here, all alone," Butch went on.

The banker nodded wary agreement. It was a point he did not feel inclined to argue.

" 'Specially if you're carrying money," Butch said. The banker shrank a little in his saddle. Were they guessing . . . ? His glance darted back and forth between them. No, they weren't guessing.

"We'll ride along with you a while," Sundance said dreamily. "Just to make sure nobody comes along—" He leaned closer to the banker, who could now see gleaming eyes in the cavern beneath the hat brim and wished that he couldn't "—and pulls out a *gun* and shoots you in the *guts* and leaves you *bleeding* in the snow to freeze to *death* and . . ."

Sundance's delivery of this exposition of the perils of the trail was impressively slow and measured. By the time he had reached this part of it, there was no need to continue; the banker had reached into his pocket, taken out a roll of bills, tossed it toward Butch, and spurred his horse into a gallop. In a moment he was lost to sight.

"Now, you see, Sundance," Butch said, after checking the money and pocketing it, "we got all our money back and that old man's got his farm. We bought a lot of goodwill, and it didn't cost a thing."

They turned their horses at a fork in the trail and kept on into the increasing snowfall. "That old man's gonna tell everyone around what a great guy Butch Cassidy is," Butch said happily.

The swirling snow almost muffled Sundance's softly spoken reply, but not—to Butch's regret—entirely. "You mean *Dutch* Cassidy."

97

CHAPTER TEN

Butch stared glumly out the window. Telluride, in the grip of winter, presented a spectacle pretty far from the glowing picture of revelry and high life he had painted for Sundance. Frame buildings, black and sodden against the waist-high snow, and a few bent figures negotiating the laboriously cut paths through it presented the only contrasts to the all-encompassing white.

He heaved a deep, mournful sigh, and turned away from the window. From his vantage point at the magnificently carved oak bar, indoor life in Telluride should have seemed a good deal more lively than the exterior view he had just abandoned. Daisy Mullen's select establishment—anyone who called it a whorehouse was considered too low class to qualify as a patron, unless he owned at least a copper mine, in which case allowances were made—seemed to hold everything a reasonable man could want in his pursuit of happiness. It afforded wine, women, and song in unlimited quantities and combinations, and in splendid surroundings. Glittering chandeliers, Venetian mirrors (some, in the bedchambers, positioned to give truly memorable effects), overstuffed plush furniture, rich wallpaper, polished floors and rugs into which you could sink to your shoetops—liquor and food from all corners of the world—knowing, agreeable women, some as opulent as the furniture, some as exciting and challenging as an unbroken bronco. Daisy's had about everything in the line of prime-grade dissipation, all right, but . . .

He looked over at the girls sprawled on the couches and settees in Daisy's "grand salon." In the daylight, they looked careless and tired, some in faded wrappers that gaped to reveal territory that usually required a fee to view; Butch knew, and they knew, that he had by now seen most of what was on display, so why bother? He was getting to be as much a fixture in this place as they were. Myra's nose was red, and she interrupted her reading of a tattered dime novel about every thirty seconds to give a deep contralto honk. Jenny, Ada, and Big Flo kept up a sort of counterpoint coughing chorus. He knew about Sierra Sue's rheumatic back—the girls seemed especially fond of talking about that—and so took it as expected that she was upstairs in her room, conserving her resources until duty called. Fellows that wrote up the glittering life of the brothel, whether from the romantic angle or coming down hard on it as sinful, Butch reflected, never seemed to consider that whores got colds, back trouble, poison ivy, and summer complaint, like everyone else. He rather wished that he were not quite so aware of all this.

The rosewood grand piano, imported, as Daisy liked to assure anyone who asked and a lot who didn't, from Austria-Hungary, where it had been played on by Strauss the Waltz King, gave off doleful atonal sounds as the tuner worked industriously at its strings.

Butch sighed again, and fished out from the best of his new suit—"latest English cut A-number-one goods," the Telluride tailor had assured him—the now somewhat bent picture the photographer Grissom had taken of him in front of the Paris backdrop, back in Steamboat Springs. *That* was a pure, honest fake, and easily worth what he'd paid. But now here he was in this elegantly appointed emporium of refined vice, surrounded by and well able to pay for women he didn't want to have anything to do with, liquor he didn't want to drink, and music he couldn't abide. He wondered if the old hardscrabble farmer whose wretched place he'd saved with the highly temporary gift of five hundred dollars, but who would still have to live with hardly any money and no prospect of getting any, was feeling, right now, as lousy as he did. He earnestly hoped so, but doubted it.

The bartender, professionally immune to the dispirited feeling that pervaded the room in daytime, drifted up to him like an amiable black thundercloud. "Can I freshen your drink, Mr. Cassidy?"

"Thank you, Jack, no," Butch said. He took two two's and a one from his vest pocket and slid them across the bar.

"What's the five dollars for, sir?" the bartender asked.

Butch looked at him and shrugged. When you were in the money, you spread it around—why else have it? Not as if it was a cowhand's thirty a month and found, with every Miss Liberty standing for what you had left for a day's hard work . . . "I don't know . . . take it."

"Thank you, sir." The bartender took the bills and looked after Butch as he walked slowly into the next room.

This Daisy had done her best to name the "petit salon"; she dropped the endeavor when it became clear that the nearest the Tellurideans were going to come to it was "pity's saloon." Now it was known simply as "t'other room," and was used for medium-sized parties or, as now, a refuge for the bored or otherwise incapable.

He found Sundance prone and somnolent on a chaise, his shoes next to him on the carpet. His gaudily shirted back was being scratched by one Lily, who was quite good-looking when not, as now, snuffling and wiping her nose. A man Butch recognized as a customer who had gone upstairs with Big Flo three nights ago lay snoring on the floor with his head propped at an awkward angle against Sundance's chaise and exhaling whiskey fumes. He had been imperfectly stuffed into his wrinkled suit, and sported a moderate stubble on his chin and jowls. Evidently Flo had kept him until he wore out, then thrown him away.

Butch sank into a chair and looked in turn at Sundance, Lily, Flo's leavings, and the four iron buckets positioned around the floor into which water plinked in irregular rhythm from leaks in the ceiling.

"I never thought I could get so sick of . . . fun after only two weeks," he said after a while.

Four widely spaced drops plinked into their receptacles before Sundance drowsily answered, "Me either."

"I need some action," Butch said.

"Me too," Sundance mumbled. He opened his eyes and twisted his head to look at his listless masseuse. "Lily . . . ?"

The girl looked down at him and was favored with a broad smile. "Not *again*," she said wearily.

"Gotta do something to keep from being bored to death," Sundance said, sliding off the chaise and standing. "Come on, let's go."

Lily sighed heavily, stood up, and slowly moved away, with Sundance following. "The things you gotta do in this job," she muttered. "Right here, okay?" She pointed at a table at the far side of the room.

"Where else?" Sundance asked.

Butch sat up in his chair.

Lily sat down, and picked up a deck of cards. Sundance slid into the chair opposite her. "Your deal," she said and shoved the cards to him.

Butch sank back, feeling somehow cheated, as Sundance began to shuffle.

The door to the grand salon slammed open; a man in a heavy coat with a green eyeshade poking incongruously from under his hat entered and peered around anxiously.

"I got a message from the Hoffman Mine that they's keelin' over like flies from the dip-theria," he said with an air of urgency.

Butch chewed on this statement for a few seconds. "Why're you telling *me*?"

"I'm tellin' him," the stranger—clearly the local telegraph man—said, pointing at the sleeping drunk. "He's the doc."

The telegrapher leaned down and shouted into the drunk's face, "We got a shipment of serum down at the express office—but it's all snowed in out at the mine, an' they ain't no way to get through!"

"You're not gettin' through to him, either," Butch observed. It seemed to him that it hardly mattered, anyhow. Drunk or sober, the doc wasn't in any shape to go any— How far was it to the Hoffman? . . . twenty-five miles or so in the snow. *Nobody* would be; the trip had to be a mankiller. And it wasn't a doctor they needed out there as much as . . .

"I been all over lookin' for volunteers," the clerk said, "but I can't find *no* takers."

Butch was about to assure him that that showed Telluride had a satisfyingly low idiot population when Daisy Mullen, sole owner and proprietor of Daisy's (and, on rare occasions when the fee warranted it, taking a more personal hand, or whatever, in the business), swept in. She was a splendidly brassy, cheerful woman, and flung Butch a fond greeting as she shook the snow from her fur-collared red coat and tossed it to a following girl. "Butch!" Lily scurried over, reached up under Daisy's skirt and began unfastening her leg warmers, something which a number of Daisy's admirers would have paid good money to be allowed to do. "Just saw a friend of yours!"

"Who?"

"Was just comin' out of the dry goods place after

givin' 'em a piece of my mind over the way they're jackin' up the prices of sheetin' on me—I mean, the way we use up sheets here, it ain't like we're some minister's household, the most wear they get is when they're washed, an' maybe an occasional Saturday night, we're entitled to a discount for *volume,* the way I see it—"

"*What* friend?"

"Oh, yah. Was comin' out of the dry goods, like I said, and I ran into O.C. Just escaped from jail, he said."

"*Hanks*?" Butch came close to yelping the name.

"You know any other O.C.'s? He asked after you, so I told him you came by here all the time."

Butch blinked. "You did." Of *course* she did, Cassidy, he told himself. Cassidy's Law. Any shit going, you get dipped in it, every time.

"He said he was lookin' forward to seein' you." Daisy flung him a brilliant smile, a dazzle of old-ivory and gold, as she proceeded up the stairs.

Butch grimaced horribly after her, then turned to the telegrapher, who was, without any great hopes, seeing if having his kidneys churned with a boot toe would arouse the doctor.

"Look," he said hurriedly. "You need somebody to take that serum up to the mine?"

"Uh, yes . . ."

"*We'll* do it!" He pointed at Sundance. "Me and him."

Sundance came off the chair like an uncoiling spring, paying no attention to the fact that one boot landed on the comatose doctor's outstretched hand, eliciting a high squeak like a chipmunk's cry. "The *hell* we will!" he yelled, knowing inside that it was no use.

Two hours later, Butch and Sundance struggled through the belly-high snow on their horses, each of which bore a canvas pack strapped behind the saddle. The horses staggered and slipped as their hoofs punched and packed snow down to icy slickness. They appeared to be attempting to learn to waltz, as well as a horse could.

"*Look,*" Sundance said. "It's one thing if we gotta get outta town because somebody's gunning for you, but give me one good reason why we're doing *this.*" He gave an indignant wave which took in the snow-field through which they were passing, the rock-fanged canyon through which they had come, and the discouraging-looking peaks which lay ahead.

"Because it's perfect."

Sundance bounced in his saddle with rage. "No, it isn't perfect. This is definitely *not* perfect! We coulda headed south, where there's *roads.*" He grabbed at his mount's mane, barely keeping himself from pitching forward over its head as it went to its knees before regaining its footing.

"Yeah," Butch said. "And Hanks could follow us just as easy. We got roads, he's got roads. What's good about this is, he'll never follow us up here."

Sundance threw him a look of dislike. "That's because *he's* smart."

Butch scooped snow out of his boottop and said, "Sundance, you're looking at it all wrong. We were bored back there, right? Well, this is an *adventure.*"

Sundance looked at his partner, back at the troughs their horses had punched through the snow, ahead at the untouched drifts and forbidding peaks, up at the sky, which seemed ready to dump another two inches on them any second, and finished the circuit with a glare at Butch.

"We can be goddamn *heroes,*" Butch said. "I mean, how often do you get a chance to *do* something for people."

"With you around," Sundance said bitterly, "too of-

104

ten. I am *sick* of you and this hero stuff. You want to be a hero, you should of gone into the Army and got your ass shot off fighting Indians or somebody."

"Now the Indians is pretty well done," Butch said, "there ain't what you could call *scope* in that. Accourse, there is something blowing up over Cuba, what I read in the papers, now McKinley's President, so there's some chances in the hero line likely to come up there. Sometimes," he mused, "I get to thinking I'd like to be a soldier of fortune, carve me out a empire in some foreign place, some sort of Spanishy country down south that hasn't got straightened out and civilized yet, where a man with ideas could make his mark. Like William Walker a long time back."

"They shot Walker," Sundance said.

Butch grinned. "Seems to be a chance you take in a lotta lines o' work, don't it?"

Sundance found nothing he felt like saying in reply to this, and instead asked, "How far is this mine?"

"Twenty-five miles."

Sundance looked at Butch anxiously. "Round trip?"

"One way."

Sundance halted his horse and slammed his fist into the side of his head in disgust. "There's no *way* we can get twenty-five miles through this stuff! It'll get deeper, further we go, and we ain't doin' a mile in an hour now. *And* we can't see the trail worth a damn, so's we could drop off into a draw an' break the horses' legs *and* our necks anytime, and . . . oh, *hell*."

Butch stopped and looked at the expanse of snowy peaks ahead. "We'll make it," he said.

"How?" Sundance asked. So did Butch, but not aloud.

With the eerie silence that accompanies a happening in a dream, a man, well muffled against the cold, slid standing across the snow in front of them. The mysteries of his presence and progress were not diminished by the incomprehensible greeting he flung back at them: "God ettermiddag!"

Butch stood up in the stirrups and called, "Hey!" The man came to a stop in a turn that threw up a cloud of snow and waited as they forced their horses to struggle toward him. When they came up to him, the man, a broad grin on his wide, windburned face, was unlashing, tightening, and retying leather thongs that held two long slats to his feet. It was obvious to Butch that these were what had kept him on top of the snow, and that the long stick he carried provided the motive power, the same idea as poling a raft upstream.

"What d'you call that?" he asked.

"Snaw-gulayding," the man said, which Butch was able to translate as "snow-gliding" after a second of working it out.

"You just go right on top of the snow like that?"

The man nodded. "Ya."

"You got any more of these things?"

"Ya. You come on to my cabin, not far, I'll show you."

Sundance shook his head in wonder. Horses weren't good enough for famed outlaw Butch Cassidy, oh, no. Some fool on barrel staves comes by, and he's ready to try *that*. The wonder was, he hadn't built himself a damn balloon to get where he was going, or worked out how to do it on a bicycle. But . . . that square-head fellow was certainly having an easier time of it getting through the snow than they were. Maybe this was one Cassidy idea that could work out. . . . He kneed his horse and followed the trough that Butch's mount had punched in the snow as it floundered after the snow-glider.

Sundance considered that Torgersen the trapper was down with a mild case of cabin fever. No normal man would be so pleased to see strangers, feed them—pots of coffee, hunks of hard bread broken from flat disks that looked like phonograph records with the small-pox, and dried-up little fish—and set about teaching them how to use the snow-gliding shoes.

But once a pair was strapped to his feet and he was able to stand upright, enthusiasm mounted in him. There was something in the way they slid on the snow, even while he was standing, as if they were just wait-ing to carry him along. . . . He gave a tentative push with the pole, and was suddenly five feet away.

"Come on, Butch!" he called. "This is great!"

Butch, just strapped onto his skis, flailed wildly, trying to keep his balance; Torgersen steadied him, grinning cheerfully.

"Wait up!" he yelled. Torgersen handed him a pole. "It looked easier when you were doing it," Butch mut-tered.

"Well, I been duing it all my life," Torgersen said modestly. He gave Butch an encouraging smile. "You pick it up fast enyuf."

Butch nodded, dug the pole firmly into the snow behind him, and expertly thrust himself face down into a drift.

"Ever-body due that a few times till they get used to the gulayding shoes," Torgersen said. "Got to ben' the knyee."

After a few minutes of instruction, Butch was able to imitate Torgersen's technique with the skis well enough to progress fairly steadily across the crust. Slide—stop—slide, getting the rhythm that worked with the pole. . . . He realized that this was one hell of a way of getting across this snowy country. How, he wondered, had a foreigner found out about it before native Americans like him and Sundance? They prob-ably studied a lot before they come over here, he fig-ured.

Sundance, now some distance off, had discovered the intoxicating joy of speed that the skis allowed. "There's nothin' to this!" he called to them, giving himself a mighty push that added appreciably to his velocity.

Torgersen cupped his hands and yelled, "Dere's a few *tricks* . . ."

Sundance was now using his pole almost as quickly as a canoer does his paddle, and moving ahead faster and faster. "Like what?" he called. "It seemed to him that he had already mastered the main thing, how to get going fast as you wanted and keep on your feet.

"Like *stopping*."

Sundance looked back with a cocky smile, then ahead. The smile froze. Just ahead of him, the slope suddenly angled down sharply, becoming an almighty steep hill. The lone snow-covered fir at the bottom looked very far away.

He dug frantically with the springy pole, but moved ahead inexorably. Then he was over the crest and going *down*.

One detached part of his mind estimated that he was now going about as fast as a good horse at the gallop, and by the time he hit the bottom of the hill he should be making something like the speed of an express train. . . .

He crouched low and dragged the pole behind him, trying to use it to steer like a flatboat's sweep. Not a damn bit of good. He reversed it in the hope that steering from the front would work better.

The result was immediate and impressive. The pole caught in the snow, dug into the pit of his stomach, and sent him pinwheeling briefly through the air. He hit with a painful thump and discovered that he could see nothing but blank whiteness, and could not move.

Either I am dead with my neck broke, he thought bitterly, or I had been buried in snow on account of these gliding shoes Butch thinks are so great. Right then, the first alternative seemed to have its good side.

From the top of the hill, Butch and Torgersen looked down at the two ski tips protruding from the snowbank which were all that could be seen of Sundance.

"One way of stopping," Butch observed.

"Dere's better." Torgersen moved to the edge of the slope and began working his way down. Butch followed, carefully copying the trapper's crabwise placement of the skis. He rehearsed what he would say to Sundance: A little accident don't mean these things aren't *good*. . . . It was your own damn fault, not listening—forget that one! . . . They're the only way we can get through. . . . Listen, it was fun for a *while*, wasn't it? That would be the line to work. . . .

CHAPTER ELEVEN

"Okay," Torgersen said the next morning. "Yure horses be okay wit' me till you come back, I got plenty feed for my pack mule, dey're welcome. Yust remember, keep yure knyees bent and don't get going no faster dan what you can stop, you make it fine. Prob'ly."

"How long you figure it should take us?" Sundance asked, adjusting his pack and bedroll on his back.

The trapper shrugged. "Ev'ryt'ing go okay, some time tomorrow, next day. A big snow or so, you got to hole up, dat'll add some. Dere's some old cabins along the way, trappers and prospectors, but they give up and move away."

"I wonder *why?*" Sundance said, looking at the jagged peaks and trackless snowfield that lay ahead of them.

The first day went fairly well, with Butch claiming substantial progress toward their goal. To Sundance, the distant peaks seemed not to have moved at all after eight hours of hard going, but there were some exhilarating moments of downhill running that made up for the tedious climbs that followed.

As Torgersen had predicted, they found an abandoned cabin in which to shelter for the night. They were bone-tired, and did not bother to cook a meal, contenting themselves with chewing some of the dried fish that the trapper had supplied them. After they wrapped themselves in their bedrolls and began to drift off, Butch got in the day's last word:

"I don't see why we shouldn't get there by maybe *noon* tomorrow, we get an early start."

Sundance could not see any reason why Butch's prediction would not come true . . . but he was pretty sure something would turn up.

When he opened his eyes the next morning, sensing that it had to be after daybreak but finding that it was still dark out, he knew what that something was. He poked his head outside to verify his suspicion, then came back and nudged Butch awake. "Forget that about noon," he said. "Grandpa of a blizzard goin' on out there. We're here till it clears, all day, anyhow."

There was enough scrap wood and rubbish in the cabin to keep a tiny fire going, and they huddled around this.

"My fingers is kind of stiff, all this cold," Sundance said; "but I expect I could handle a deck of cards. You want to break 'em out, Butch? Something to pass the time?"

"I, uh, didn't bring any cards."

Sundance sighed. "Well, seeing as we're not gonna have to be in top shape today for hard traveling, I s'pose we could warm ourselves up with a couple shots an' forget our troubles a while."

"Uh . . ."

"You didn't bring any whiskey," Sundance said flatly.

"Well, no. I didn't expect . . ."

Sundance looked around the dilapidated cabin, at the feeble fire, at the storm outside, at their bedrolls and packs. "I want to get this straight," he said gently. "You was *bored* at Daisy's. All them women, that bar with everything you ever *heard* of in it, three casinos down the street to try your luck at, that was *boring* you. An' *this* is an adventure."

"Well . . ." Butch began defensively, then stopped. Once he had said that, it struck him that he had already used up his strongest talking point.

"I'm not *arguing*," Sundance said. "I just want to be sure I *understand*. I guess it takes a while to get the hang of adventuring when you ain't used to it. If I can stand the excitement, I b'lieve I'll go on back to sleep. Lemme know when the storm stops making it adventuresome outside, huh?"

As Sundance drifted off into a morose sleep, he heard the mournful sounds of Butch's harmonica approximating "My Old Kentucky Home." Pleasant to think about some place—*any* place—far away, where the sun was shining bright . . . .if only Butch could get the notes right. . . .

A long glide over fresh powder snow carried them a quarter of a mile in a few minutes. They stopped and grimly prepared for the next awkward, grueling passage up the incline in front of them. The fun was gone out of those fast runs now, spoiled by the prospect of what every easy bit of progress had waiting at the end of it: the painstaking placement of the skis, stretching muscles they'd never used; the growing weight of their packs rubbing shoulders and collarbones raw; the itchy, damp heat of their bodies during such exertion, which didn't carry over at all to mitigate the icy cold that tormented their exposed faces.

"Wait'll we get to Hoffman's, Sundance," Butch said with forced cheerfulness. "They're not gonna *believe* it when they see us."

Sundance said nothing, but glared at his partner.

Butch made an extravagant gesture with his pole, which came close to costing him his balance. "We'll come gliding in there with this serum and they'll cheer and carry *on*. . . ." He looked dreamily ahead. "You know what? They'll have a parade! They'll probably name stuff after us . . . Cassidy Creek . . ."

Sundance poled himself stolidly ahead. "Sundance Cemetery . . ."

"You know," Butch said after a moment, "you're a really *cheerful* guy to travel with."

Topping the crest of a pass, Sundance put on a burst of speed and swept past Butch. It was easier this time than when he'd tried it before. The mighty Cassidy seemed to be running out of steam. That's what a *planner* does, he confided to himself, sets a thing going without making sure that he's got the stuff to see it through. Well, Mister Planner Cassidy (well known in parts of Utah) can just hump himself to catch up. Shouldn't take much doing, though; I'm about done, too. Sundance stopped. Had that been a sound, a call, or what? He looked back toward the distant figure of his partner.

"Sundance . . ."

Butch staggered more than skied the last yards between them. He pulled himself briefly out of his crouching stance, then lost his footing and dropped into a snowbank. He lay gasping for breath, his teeth chattering.

"Okay," Sundance said unfeelingly. "That's enough of a rest. Let's get moving."

Butch twisted on the surface of the snow and tried to lever himself up with his arms, then fell back. "I can't . . ."

Sundance bent over him and caught him under the arms. "Leg cramps?"

Butch shook his head. "My legs went dead two hours ago." He looked up at Sundance. "I'm freezing . . ."

Sundance looked down at his partner's slick-beaded forehead. "*Freezing*? You're sweating."

"Head aches," Butch mumbled. "Throbbing . . ."

"Jesus," Sundance said. "I bet you've got it."

"Got . . . what?"

"Diphtheria."

Butch shook his head feebly. "No . . ."

"*What* then?" Sundance demanded. "*Gotta* be it. You must of caught it from one of the girls." He looked at Butch reflectively. "First time any one of 'em ever gave anybody *diphtheria*."

He slid one arm around Butch and tried to haul him upright. Heavy lifting while wearing skis had not been in Torgersen's short course of instruction, and Sundance found himself atop the man he had been attempting to help, pressing him further down into the snow. He rolled away and lay on his back for a moment, breathing heavily.

"I'm not gonna make it," Butch said, each word an effort. "You gotta keep going, Sundance. Save yourself . . . leave me here."

Sundance snapped up to a sitting position and glared at Butch.

"No . . . really. No use . . . both of us . . . dying."

Sundance slammed his hand onto the snow crust. "You'd *love* that, wouldn't you! You'd be a *real* hero then. Dead heroes are the best kind, right?"

Butch, half immersed in the snow, looked up at the leaden sky. His fingers made plucking movements as if he were trying to pull up a coverlet. He spoke in a long sigh: "Shut up . . ."

"You're really *happy* about this, aren't you!" Sundance yelled. "You can see it right now—a big *monument* right out here. 'Here lies Butch Cassidy, outlaw an' hero, who died trying to carry serum to sick children an' dogs'!"

"Shut . . . *up,* Sundance."

Sundance glared wildly around. "Well, the hell with that! You're not gonna be a hero at my expense. You're gonna keep going whether you like it or not!"

"I . . . can't."

"Yes, you *can!*" Sundance thrashed around, trying to slip the straps of his pack from his shoulders. "Because we've got the goddam serum! We're carrying it right on our backs!" He got the pack off and down on the snow in front of him. With numbed fingers he attacked the buckles and finally extracted a bottle of clear liquid, one of four, which he held up triumphantly.

"Here you go!" he said. "Drink it."

Butch raised his head and said impatiently, "You don't *drink* serum, you dumb bastard."

"What, then?"

"I saw a doc do it once," Butch said, gaining interest in the proceedings, now that there seemed some possible alternative to a heroic death. "He had some kind of a glass tube . . . with this needle thing."

"Needle?"

"Yes. And he stuck it in this guy's arm."

Sundance shook his head as he rummaged in the pack. What medicine was, it was when you took some pills or a tonic, or got a cut sewed up or a bullet dug out of you or a bone set, nothing to do with *needles* and *tubes* and such. But . . . there, just the way Butch had said, were a couple of glass tubes with plungers at one end and godalmighty sharp-looking points at the other. These had to be them. He held them up for Butch to see.

Butch nodded. "You gotta get the serum in the glass tube."

Sundance looked from the hypodermics to the serum bottle and back. "How?"

"I don't know."

Sundance nodded. *Naturally* Butch wouldn't know. He would know about serums, about these needle things, sure. But when it came to how you got one into the other, why, that'd be one of them trifling details that your man with the broad view of things wouldn't be up on.

He pulled at one of the plungers and found that it came out of the tube with a sharp *thwock* sound. He smiled triumphantly at Butch. That was half the job. Now all that was left was to get the glop *in* there. And after that, jam the needle into someplace on Butch, ram the plunger home, and let the serum do whatever it was supposed to.

Sundance managed to unscrew the cap from the serum bottle with fingers that had about as much feeling as twigs, except for hurting like hell, but that was his last success. His hands were shaking from the cold, and his first try at dribbling the serum from the bottle into the open tube sent almost half of it to form a wet stain on the snow. The serum, maybe because of the cold, was as slow-running as molasses, and the tube of the hypodermic syringe was bafflingly narrow. The stuff ran down the side of the bottle, onto his fingers, into the snow—almost everywhere, in fact, except into the syringe. He shifted his grip on the bottle in a try for greater control; slippery now from its spilled contents, it slipped from his grasp and emptied itself into the snow.

"You almost got it," Butch said weakly. "Try again."

Sundance fished the nearly empty bottle out of the snow and held it to the syringe tube again. But his hands chattered the bottle against the tube, no matter how hard he tried to hold them steady; the only result was another drip of the thick fluid down the side of the syringe. He stood up and furiously hurled the bottle as far as he could.

He yelled down at Butch, "You *would* get sick! You would get us out here on this dumb stunt and then you get *sick* on me!"

Butch looked up at Sundance's accusing stare. That partnership he'd been so set on, it struck him, hadn't worked out quite the way he'd planned. One way or another, it seemed about to break up.

"I should just *leave* you here."

"That's what I told you."

"Go to hell."

Butch closed his eyes. That seemed like about the only instruction he was up to following. When the ravages of the disease had left him a lifeless corpse, as the papers would probably put it—would Sundance struggle back to civilization with the whole pathetic story?—it didn't seem likely that there would be any pearly gates and harps in his future. . . .

His eyes snapped open. "What was that?"

Sundance opened his mouth to speak. Butch waved him to silence, straining to listen. Yes, there was something. . . . "You hear that?"

Now Sundance caught the distant murmur of human voices, muffled by the falling snow. He faced the direction they seemed to be coming from and yelled, "Hey!"

An answering call came back, unintelligible but unmistakable. Now the voices were closer. Sundance and Butch—up on one elbow and alert again—peered through the snow.

"We're over here!" Sundance called.

Shadows appeared in the white, then materialized into a group of six men dragging something behind them.

"Hot damn!" Sundance muttered. "Maybe we hit a supply party for the mine, Butch. Think they might have a bottle or so with them? I could use a drink about now. An' listen, they could help get that serum stuff into you, you'll be *okay* in no—"

He stopped as the men's burden became more clearly visible.

A long toboggan being pulled through the snow . . . and on it a long wooden box. A coffin.

The procession stopped and the heavily muffled group looked curiously at the two men, one upright and leaning on his ski pole, the other half buried in a drift.

117

Sundance looked at the coffin. "Maybe that's for you," he muttered to Butch. He struggled toward the party, calling out, "We brought serum." He looked expectantly at the men. That cheering and carrying on Butch had talked of didn't really mean anything to him, but now that it was time for it, he might as well get some. God knew he'd earned it.

The men—several of them, he could see now, were only boys, one no more than ten—stared back at him emotionlessly.

Quite some cheering and carrying on, Sundance thought. "We came all the way from Telluride to bring it!" he said.

One of the men finally spoke. "Why didn't you get here sooner?"

"*Sooner!*" Storms, freezing, nearly dying, learning to use these damn gliding shoes . . . sooner!

"We been asking for help near a week," another man said.

Sundance gripped his ski pole and took a step toward the man, snarling, "You sonofabitch, he nearly died!" He pointed at Butch.

"*She* did die," the first man said wearily.

"Who did?" Butch asked.

The man pointed to the coffin. "My wife." He nodded toward the boys. "Their mother."

Sundance slumped, holding the pole for support. He and Butch looked dully at the burial party. Adventure for us, he thought. Not for these poor bastards, though.

When the grim task of interment in the frozen ground was completed, the mourners lashed Butch to the now-vacant toboggan along with his and Sundance's packs and their skis, and began the trudge back to the mine. "We can give him the injection there," the widower said briefly to Sundance. "He should make it okay." He resumed his place at the head of the party.

Sundance, trudging alongside the toboggan, looked down with a disgusted expression. "Well, you got your parade, Butch."

CHAPTER TWELVE

In spite of the dourness of his greeting, Hoffman, the mine owner who had lost his wife, and his sons tended Butch efficiently, and eventually expressed some gratitude for the arrival of the serum; it did, after all, cure the remaining cases of diphtheria among the mine workers.

"Don't suppose, bein' fair," he observed to Sundance, "you could of made it much quicker."

"Not knowin' the country, being hit with a couple of blizzards, no way for a horse to get through, studying how to use them gliding shoes without falling down or dropping into a hole under the snow, and Butch coming down with the diphtheria—no, I don't see as we could of," Sundance said.

"If it was your wife sick, then dyin', I guess you'd know how I felt," Hoffman said.

"Ain't married, either of us," Sundance remarked. Butch, on a cot in the corner of the room, stirred uneasily, and Sundance went to get a dipper of water for him.

"You'll be ready to get on outta here anytime, Butch," he said. "Mending fast, so they tell me. Now the thaw's started, there's be a pack train going down to Telluride, an' they'll take us. I'll peel off at Torgersen's an' get the horses, so's there won't be nothing for you to bother yourself about."

"Yeah," Butch said. "But what about O.C.?"

Sundance shrugged. "That's one bridge we'll have to burn when we get to it."

Butch sat up, his eyes bright with thought. "What we do is, we get the pack train to let us off just at the edge of town—get the horses from Torgersen some other time, we better stick together. That ratty little place just when you get there, Ryan's, the guys that hang out there'll be sure to know where O.C.'s at, so we can ask around and plan according." He frowned. "Of course, O.C. might just be *there*, so I gotta think of a way to get around that. . . ."

Sundance shook his head. Butch was for sure getting well now, planning away like crazy.

The elaborate caution of their return to Telluride proved to be unnecessary. "O.C. went out a couple days ago," Daisy informed them. "Hired on as a mule driver soon as the thaw came and the roads south opened up. There was a lot coming through on the telegraph about him, and some of the boys that likes to reside here in comfort give him the word he might be happier somewheres else. A man that's just busted out of the pen draws too much law around a place, they told him, so the only way it'd be convenient all around for him to stay would be six foot under. He got the idea, at least soon's they tried speaking into his good ear, an' took out. Said he was awful sorry to have missed you, Butch, but he'd be careful not to, next time your trails crossed."

"Good of him," Butch said.

The aftereffects of Butch's bout with diphtheria lingered, or so he claimed to Sundance, with frequent dramatic coughs. When Sundance suggested that he consult the local doctor, he shuddered. "Dead drunk most of the time, you remember? Don't know as he's moved from the floor in the pity saloon for a week. Might be dead, for all I know. No, I gotta look me up a first-class medical man, which there ain't none of nearer than Denver."

"Ain't you wanted for that bank robbery in Denver?"

"Sure . . . but not wanted very *much*, that being old history now. We don't advertise ourselves, they're not gonna bother us. We'll just slip nice and quiet from the train station to the nearest doc's and—"

"*Train* station?"

Butch spread his hands. "Sure. We got to go on this trip, we might as well do it in style."

Sundance nodded sardonically. Butch was ailing, all right, but not from the disease. Telluride was getting to him. Well, so it was to Sundance—what the hell. . . .

"This is the *life*," Butch said dreamily, watching the snow-covered mountains glide past and sipping a highball. Sundance, in the plush chair opposite him, was obliged to agree that it beat a good number of their recent experiences.

"Clean, comfortable bunks," Butch mused. "Get up when you want to, stroll down to the dining car, get shaved, write letters, just sit here in the chair car and relax, let the world go by outside them windows. *Look* at that—we just came by a stretch in five minutes that'd be *hours* on a horse."

"Or on them gliding shoes," Sundance agreed.

"Hey, porter!" Butch called. When the blue-coated attendant came up, he said, "If you're not too busy, would you get me another of these?" He held out his glass. "How about you, Sun—uh, Fred?"

"Not just now, uh, Sam," Sundance said. It didn't come easy to him to use the fake names Butch had insisted on their using. Fred Smith and Sam Jones didn't strike him as much of a disguise.

"Certainly, sir," the porter said, smiling. He was a middle-aged black man with a neat moustache. "Not busy at all right now, you gentlemen being the only

122

passengers in the chair car, and I've made up the berths for the day. A pleasure, sir."

When the man returned with his fresh highball, Butch said, "Say, porter. I bet you get lots of interesting passengers along this run. Maybe some big-time gamblers, badmen, outlaws? That must make things exciting."

"I believe I have noticed some like that," the porter said. "But we don't pay attention to such matters. If a gentleman is a Pullman passenger, he's entitled to service, and that's what we see he gets. What he may have been doing before he boarded or what he plans to do when he leaves us—why, we don't trouble ourselves about that so long as he's gentlemanly while on board."

"You ever recall anybody like . . . oh, Butch Cassidy traveling with you?"

The porter shook his head. "I'm afraid I don't know the name, sir."

"Oh." Butch glared at the grinning Sundance. "Well, there must be some, uh, colorful characters traveling this line?"

The porter gave him a long look; a slight smile flickered under the moustache. "Well, sir . . . is the name of Deadwood Dick familiar to you?"

"Sure!" Butch said. "One hell of a cowboy, buffalo hunter, top gunfighter, Indian fighter. Won a roping contest thirty years back, set a record that hasn't been beat yet. Not an outlaw, but some of his gunfights put him mighty close to it—he would of *been* an outlaw after some scrape I heard of in a border cantina if they were counting Mexicans in those days. Deadwood Dick, yeah . . . one of the real tough hombres . . . uh, colored man, wasn't he?"

The porter nodded. "Yes, sir. Born a slave, in fact, went west when he was sixteen."

"Haven't heard anything about him in years, seems to me. You say he rides this line often?"

"Very often, sir."

"What do you know?" Butch leaned toward Sundance. "Now, Fred, you ought to pay attention to this. You don't hardly know *anything* about the really famous people, the ones that've built up a reputation that stands for years. I bet old Dick's got himself a spread someplace where everybody for miles around looks up to him an' asks him to tell all his stories." He shook his head admiringly at the vision.

Sundance looked at the porter. "That the way it is with this Deadwood Dick fellow?"

"Not quite, sir."

"Pretty well off, though?" Butch asked. "I mean, he can afford to ride in Pullman all the time, that takes something of a roll."

"Not if you're paid to do it, sir. With the salary and tips, I find it works out very comfortably. Another drink, sir? Thank you, sir."

When the porter had gone, Butch and Sundance looked intently out the window, carefully avoiding each other's gaze.

After some moments, Sundance said reflectively, "Well . . . it beats winding up with a bullet in your gut."

Butch looked at him savagely.

"Well, don't it?"

"Just shut the hell *up!*"

Sundance grinned. "Sure, Sam."

"You're sound as a dollar, Mr. Jones," the doctor said as Butch rebuttoned his shirt and attached his collar and tie.

"I kind of figured he might be," Sundance said from where he lounged in a chair at the far side of the office.

"You can't be too careful, can you, though, Doctor?" Butch said, knotting his tie.

"Quite right. And, while I'm glad to say that you

have no remaining ill effects from your case of diphtheria—you were very fortunate in having such ready access to a supply of serum as you evidently had—" Sundance snorted. "—I should point out that you ought to watch your weight. You are beginning to acquire a touch of adiposity about the abdomen which reflects inaction and may in time become a problem."

"Thank you, Doctor," Butch said stiffly. "I'll keep that in mind."

The doctor looked at him. "Have you consulted me before, Mr. Jones? There's something familiar about your face."

"I don't believe so. I'm not in Denver much. Me and my partner, we're just briefly down . . . from Canada."

"Ah. Well," the doctor said with a tight smile, "forgive my mentioning it, but I do hope you don't intend to pay the, ah, consultation fee in Canadian currency. We're not equipped—"

"Good old U.S. dollars, Doc," Butch said. "How much?" He brought out a roll of bills and stood waiting to count out whatever might be called for. The doctor's eyes went from Butch's hands holding the money to his face and back again, then widened.

"Wait a minute," he said. "I know where . . . I was making a deposit at the First National when you . . . yes, you're the one . . . Butch Cassidy!" His hand darted toward the telephone on his desk.

"*Somebody* finally heard of you," Sundance drawled. "Make you happy? *Freeze*, Doc!"

The doctor looked into the muzzle of Sundance's revolver, and his hand, as if possessing independent life, crept away from the telephone and huddled on the desk like a frightened spider.

"I . . . I won't say anything," the doctor squeaked.

"*Accourse* you won't," Sundance said genially, centering the pistol between the doctor's eyes, which promptly closed as he turned pale.

"Sundance," Butch said severely. "You're forgetting the noise."

"That's so. Wouldn't do to disturb all the sick folks in your waiting room, now, would it?" He felt that he must be getting a taste for this adventure stuff. Here they were on some damn-fool errand in Denver, with Butch recognized and the law about to be on their tails, no way around that, most of their money in safe-keeping with Daisy back in Telluride . . . and, damn it, he was *enjoying* it!

The doctor's cupboard provided rolls of gauze bandage with which Butch expertly trussed him to his chair. The doctor mustered up courage enough to say, "You can't leave me here like this. There are sick people out there needing to see me."

Butch folded a pad of gauze and squeezed it experimentally. Solid enough to form an effective gag, wide enough so it wouldn't slip into his throat and choke him. "They're sick enough, they'll bust in and see you."

The doctor shook his head. "You don't know Nurse Atkins. She'd let somebody die of snakebite right in the waiting room sooner than let a patient in before I'd called for him."

"So," Butch said interestedly. With deft fingers he slipped the gag into the doctor's mouth and secured it with a gauze strip tightly knotted at the back of his neck.

"Well," he said heartily to Sundance. "Guess we'd better be on our way. The McCartys'll be waiting for us in San Antone, and we'll have to make tracks to get there in time."

The doctor's eyes narrowed, and the gag twitched as if he were silently mouthing something, such as "San Antonio," in order to memorize it. Sundance gave Butch a long look.

They stepped outside, careful to screen the interior of the office from any gaze. Butch stopped at the desk

126

and said to the grim-faced woman in white who sat there, "Doctor asked me to tell you he's not to be disturbed—not on *any* account—for . . . twenty minutes. He's on the telephone, urgent consultation about an epidemic of the epizootic that has just broke out."

"Twenty minutes," the woman said, with a pleased look at the several sufferers in the waiting room.

Outside, as Butch set off down the street at a quick pace, Sundance said, "Lemme see. That about Santone was to throw him off our trail? I mean, we ain't *going* there?"

Butch shook his head. "Hell, no. We head straight west for as far as our money'll take us an' leave enough left over to get a couple of horses an' gear. They'd nab us *quick* if we went back to Telluride for the rest of our cash, damn it."

"An' another thing," Sundance said, hurrying to keep up with Butch. "We could of got out of Denver without all this rush if you'd just told that damn woman the doc wanted an *hour* to himself. Why the twenty minutes?"

"Well . . ." Butch looked at him abashedly. "Somebody *might* of had the snakebite."

CHAPTER THIRTEEN

Ten days later, and some hundreds of miles to the west, Sundance delightedly savored the intense blue sky and the dazzling white field of wild daisies through which they were riding, and the brilliant rocks of the canyon wall to their left. Spring was goddam here at last! Good-bye snow, good-bye Telluride, good-bye diseases and serums and gliding shoes—the whole lousy winter was behind them (including, but what the hell, the cash they'd gone into it with; just *maybe* Daisy would have it for them if they ever dropped back there), and he and Butch had the whole damn *world* in front of them, ready for the taking.

"Let's get us a *train!*" he said happily.

Butch looked thoughtful. "Trains take a hell of a lot of planning."

"Well, that's your end of things, ain't it? Plan away, then lead me to it an' watch my smoke."

"You gotta coordinate everything, you gotta know schedules, you need four men at the least. Try it with fewer'n that, and you wind up in a spot where you got to balance yourself on your ass an' tote guns with both hands and one foot, which don't leave you much chance to pick up what you're after in the first place, that being the money."

They stopped and dismounted at the sparkling creek that ran near the edge of the brightly colored canyon wall; their horses drank gratefully and noisily.

"I guess we throwed off all pursuit, like they say,"

Sundance remarked. "That was some slick, the way you whisked us out of Denver, an' everybody expecting us to head for Santone 'stead of Utah."

"I hope so," Butch said. "What you really got to count on, something like that, is that they ain't awfully *interested*. I mean, they got better things to do than follow up some old bank robbery an' a complaint by a doctor that's had his feathers ruffled some and lost twenty minutes of office time. If anybody was really hot after us, that wouldn't of done all that much good."

He turned to Sundance earnestly. "You see, that's it. You got to know what to expect out of a situation, how it works, study things out ahead of time. Like when Matt Warner and me robbed the Denver and Rio Grande in '87 or so. Stopped it real easy, opened up the express car like *that*—" he snapped his fingers "—put in a charge of dynamite on *top* of the safe. We didn't *know* any better, see, just dumber'n hell then—and set it off."

He grinned and shook his head. "Blew the damn safe right through the floor of the car."

Sundance returned the grin, then frowned. He cut his eyes toward the canyon wall.

"Wedged 'er right between the tracks under the car," Butch continued. "Couldn't get *at* it, couldn't move the train . . ."

"So you *left* it?" Sundance muttered, giving Butch only half his attention and quickly scanning the rocks at the top of the canyon.

Butch nodded. "Might still be there, for all I know." He glanced at Sundance, suddenly registering his alertness. "What is it?"

"Act like nothin's wrong," Sundance muttered, "but sorta move over toward that grove over there. . . ."

A twig snapped behind them. They crouched and dove for cover behind the nearest rocks, almost in midair as a gunshot slammed, sending echoes down the canyon.

Butch rolled, crouched behind his chosen rock, and drew his gun.

From the grove a grating voice called, "That's for turning me in, you bastard!"

Still keeping well behind the rock, Butch lifted his voice. "O.C., is that you?" There was no reply; Butch supposed there really didn't have to be, given the circumstances. *"I didn't turn you in!"* Again no reply. Well, what the hell was he expecting: "That so, Butch? Gee, I'm sorry I misjudged you?"

"O.C.?"

After a moment he heard from the grove the sound of a horse riding away. He sighed, reholstered his gun, and stood up. He looked toward where he had seen Sundance scooting to get behind a rock. "Bad enough," he complained, "having to watch out for the law, but when your own *men* are gunning for you . . ." He stopped. Sundance seemed to be no more communicative than O.C. And where was he, anyhow?

"Sundance?"

"Yeah . . . ?" The voice came weakly. Butch ran toward it and found Sundance near the edge of the carpet of wild daisies, on his knees, and holding his hands as if he'd had a sudden stomachache.

Butch bent over him. "What happened?"

"He missed you," Sundance whispered, "and nicked *me.*"

"Lemme see."

His jaw went stiff as he saw the dark blood seeping from between Sundance's clenched fingers.

Sundance gave him a slack smile. His eyes were unfocused. "I've never been wounded in all the gunfights I been in . . . isn't that funny?" he said.

"You'll be *okay,*" Butch said heartily. "There's a good doctor in Circleville. It's not that far, maybe thirty miles. Can you make it?"

Sundance closed his eyes a second, then opened them. "Easy."

For the first few miles, Butch was able to tell himself that Sundance was right. The kid was tough as whang leather—hadn't he made that epic trip to the Hoffman mine without faltering? A bullet could slow him up, but he'd hold out as far as Circleville, long as they didn't try anything foolish like galloping, of course he would. Just on sunset now, they'd have to go slow anyhow. . . .

"Got to . . . stop a minute," Sundance said, gasping the words out with difficulty. Butch could see the stain widening on the front of his shirt, extending beyond the spread hand that covered the wound.

"Okay." Butch reined his horse in, then reached over and pulled Sundance's to a halt.

". . . get down . . ."

Butch nodded, dismounted, and moved quickly toward Sundance, catching him just as he began a slow topple from the saddle. The jolt drew a sharp intake of breath from Sundance, but no groan. Butch lowered him gently to the ground, stripped off his own jacket, folded it, and slid it under Sundance's head.

"We . . . gotta stop the bleeding," Sundance mumbled.

Butch nodded, unbuttoned his shirt and slid out of it. He grabbed the tail and started to tear a strip from it.

"That won't do it . . . bandages no good."

"*How*, then?"

Sundance took a deep breath and winced at the pain it cost him. "Haah . . . Take a bullet . . ."

"A bullet," Butch said, his eyes narrowing. He took a cartridge from his gunbelt and held it up so that Sundance could see it.

"Yeah . . . go on, break it open."

Butch looked at him questioningly. "Uh . . ."

"There's . . . tool in my saddlebag."

Rummaging, Butch found something like a small wrench. It looked as if it might be good for pulling the nose out of a cartridge; anyhow, it didn't look good for anything else. He twisted the lead slug out with surprising ease, and went back to Sundance, holding the open cartridge. "Okay."

"Sprinkle the powder around the wound."

Butch hesitated and frowned. "Look, are you *sure* you want—"

"*Do* it!"

Butch pulled the blood-sticky shirt open, winced at the sight of the oozing hole in the pale flesh, and scattered the grains of black powder around and into it. Something new every day, he thought. Used to say spiderwebs were good for stanching wounds, but gunpowder . . . He hoped it would work; anyhow, it was done. "Okay."

"Now . . . light it."

Butch snapped upright. "*What!*"

"Get a match and light it."

"No!"

"Then give me a match and I'll do it myself," Sundance said wearily.

"No! Damned if I will!" Butch's flesh seemed to crawl at the thought.

"It's the only way to stop the blood. If you don't do it, I'm gonna bleed to death!"

"*Sundance,*" Butch said urgently, "it's gonna hurt like *hell*—it could kill you!"

"It already hurts like hell . . . and it's gonna kill me for *sure* if you don't—"

"Okay!" Butch said. He clenched his teeth. What the hell kind of world was it where a man was willing to take his chances to get what he wanted, face up to lawmen and such, but wound up having to burn his best friend alive to keep his guts from bleeding away? It seemed to be the world he was in. . . . "Okay."

132

The horrible decision taken, the next thing was to carry it out, but: "I don't have a match."

Sundance slid a hand into his trousers pocket, pulled out a wooden, sulphur-headed match, and held it up. Butch grimaced, took it, and, forcing himself not to hesitate, struck it on a rock.

It flared in the gathering dusk, stinging his nostrils with a sharp smell, then dwindled to an unsteady flame—unsteady because the hand that held it quivered.

Sundance, looking at the burning match with a mixture of horror and hope, whispered, "If you don't do it fast, you're gonna shake it out."

Butch took a deep breath. Sundance squeezed his eyes shut and gritted his teeth, waiting for—

There was a brief blink of light in the gloom, like a photographer's flash-powder holder illuminating a night picture, a sudden smell of scorched meat, and a wild, inhuman scream that rose and died away in a short second as unconsciousness mercifully claimed the man who had uttered it.

Butch, shaken and spent as if he had run ten miles through rocky country, hunkered next to Sundance. All *right*, he told himself, you didn't want to do it, but you done it. And *he* was man enough to take it. So the next thing is to get him someplace to be taken care of. The doc in Circleville? Too far, now. And, come to think of it, likely to be some touchy about treating gunshot wounds without a word to the sheriff.

Well . . . there was a nearer place.

CHAPTER FOURTEEN

. . . a face . . . gentle, pretty . . . angel? . . . if so,
a surprise . . . bending over . . . mouth moving . . .
"Are you . . . feeling . . ."
. . . saying something . . . what . . . here goes
again . . . sinking . . .

Sundance lay on the bed with his eyes closed and
frowned. He was Harry Alonzo Longabaugh; he was
clear on that point. And something awful had happened to him a while back, just what it was would
come back to him in a bit. But just where he was and
when it was, those matters were a little beyond him
right now. It was as if, a second or so ago, something
had switched him on again like an electric light, but
without the full current getting through. There was
something about an angel, or at least a woman who
looked mighty like one, saying something to him,
somewhere in a misty past. . . . And, in the present,
he realized, a damn *big* housefly or some such perched
on his lip.

His eyes still closed, he reached up a hand to brush
it away. It didn't move when he touched it; in fact, it
felt like—

His eyes snapped open. The first thing they saw was
rough-sawed ceiling boards above him. He rolled them
cautiously and was rewarded with the sight of a
shaded window, the top of a chest of drawers, and . . .

the grave but placid face of a woman seated on a cane chair next to him.

He closed his eyes, opened them again, and decided that she must have been the one he'd seen in his dream, or whatever it was. A face that had seen some wear, but strong and handsome, for all that. In fact, downright pretty. Her own woman, and good luck for the man she decided to share herself with.

Sundance was beginning to get it all back again— Butch, the ride through the meadow of daisies, the seminar on robbing trains, the sudden shot that had gone through him like a red-hot poker, the ride, the growing weakness, the . . . *that* part he'd look into a little later, thanks.

He studied the woman with interest, and gave her his best smile.

"You're looking much better," she said.

Sundance thought of saying that she didn't look so bad herself, but that seemed too much like an opening move with one of the girls at Daisy's. He was also unsure, until he had tried speaking, that he could get the sentence out as clearly as he would have liked. It seemed to him that it must have been an awfully long time since he'd said anything.

"You need washing up," the woman said.

Sundance was pleased. He didn't feel especially dirty, but if this good-looking woman wanted to sponge him down all over, why argue? "Okay," he croaked. Out of practice, but he'd get the hang of speaking again, when there was reason to, which looked like coming about pretty soon.

The woman left the room, and Sundance propped himself up on his elbows and looked around it. Chest of drawers, washstand, small mirror, unpapered walls. The most impressive item of furniture was the bed he was lying in. Just where the hell *was* he?

The woman came back into the room, carrying a

kettle, from which she poured steaming water into the bowl on the washstand. She lifted the bowl and brought it over to the small table by the bed.

"What's your name?" Sundance said.

"Mary." She dipped a rough-textured cloth into the hot water, wrung it out, and washed his face gently but efficiently. "Where is this?"

"About ten miles from Circleville," Mary said. "You shouldn't talk too much."

Actions speak louder than words, Sundance thought complacently as she pulled down the sheet, uncovering his torso. He cocked his head and saw a bandage, reassuringly clean-looking, covering the spot where O.C. had shot him. He bore O.C. Hanks no ill will, but there was no denying that it would be an entertaining spectacle to see what a bunch of Apache squaws might do to him, beginning with slicing his eyelids off, and going on to that stuff they did with fire ants. . . .

The smooth, soothing slide of the hot wet cloth over his chest, side, and abdomen brought his thoughts away from O.C. and focused them quite sharply on the here-and-now. He looked with fascination as Mary's hand, holding the cloth, described circles on his body, closer and closer to where the sheet had been folded down. That was *some* friendly hand, and no mistake. He glanced up from it and caught her eye.

Mary looked back at him with a steady, grave glance. Sundance was sure that his mouth had not been that dry a second ago. . . .

She stood up. "I'll tell him you're awake."

Sundance gulped. "Tell him in an *hour*," he said hoarsely.

She gave him a look he could not understand—unless a combination of "Yes," "Never," "Sorry," "Some other time," and "You shithead" made sense—and left the room.

Sundance lay there smirking. Not now, okay, he told himself. But you gotta admit that there's what you call the old spark there. . . . He heard a quick exchange between Mary's voice and a deeper one outside the room, then Butch strode in, grinning.

"The doctor said you're gonna make a *total* recovery," Butch said expansively. He did not go into the strange tale of Sundance's carelessness in dropping a cartridge into a cook fire and sustaining a one-in-a-million wound that he had been obliged to foist on the Circleville medico in order to avoid inconvenient questions from the law.

"How long've I been out?"

Butch unhooked the mirror from the nail which supported it on the wall and carried it over, holding it in front of Sundance's face.

"*That's* how long."

Sundance saw the accustomed collection of features, enhanced by a full moustache. For a moment he felt like that old-time fellow in the book they'd had in school, that went out bowling with some Dutchmen, and lost his way home or something. Rip, Rap, some name like that. But there was no denying it added something. Fellow with a moustache like that, nobody's gonna call *him* Alonzo; it *goes* with a handle like the Sundance Kid.

"We thought it'd be a nice present for you when you finally came to," Butch said. "Mary shaved you and shaped it up real nice like that."

Sundance fingered the ends of the moustache. Was it going to need waxing? Better just let it droop at the ends, but it'd be a good idea to get a pair of clippers or scissors to keep it even. Nothing worse than a messy moustache that caught all kinds of food and suchlike in it . . . Was it better for women for a man to have a moustache, worse, or didn't they care? Could be he'd be getting some information on that point pretty soon. . . .

"Listen, Butch," he said conspiratorially. "About Mary . . . ?"

137

Butch eyed him. "What about her?"

Sundance leaned over on one elbow and half-lowered one eyelid. "If you hadn't come in, I think I could of . . . you know."

Butch thrust his thumbs into the waistband of his trousers, rocked back on his heels, squinted at the ceiling, and then favored the floor with a studious look. After a moment he shook his head and said thoughtfully, "It's better you didn't. In your condition and all."

Sundance glanced down at the folded sheet that covered the lower half of his body. "As far as *condition* goes—"

"Besides," Butch said, with a smile a little too broad to be genuine, "she's my wife."

Sundance slept deeply, peacefully. If his dreams touched upon certain situations involving his partner's wife, there was nobody to reproach him for that.

The door to the bedroom creaked open, and feet scuffled on the floor, a few feet above which a kerosense lamp, turned low so that only a fingernail paring of flame quivered on the end of the wick, was borne along slowly.

The light fell on Sundance's face. His eyelids flickered; before they were fully open, he had whipped his revolver out from under his pillow, leveled at two very wide-eyed little boys in overalls and wool shirts.

One nine, one seven, he figured. What the hell. They come for me, I could beat 'em bare-knuckle, tads like that. He slid the gun back under the pillow.

The kids kept staring at him with those big eyes glinting in the soft lantern light, the way you'd think he was some elephant or two-headed calf at a county fair side show. "Whaddaya want?" he said gruffly.

"Are you really the Sundance Kid?" the older asked in awed tones.

Sundance nodded. Unless this kid was a midget lawman, the admission seemed safe enough.

"Who are you?" he asked.

"Robert LeRoy Parker, Junior, sir."

Sundance turned to the younger one.

"I'm Sam." His brother dug him in the ribs with an elbow. "Uh—Samuel Maximilian Parker, sir."

Sundance considered them for a moment. Butch's kids . . . and damn if he'd even known Butch had so much as a wife. And how had Butch come to use *Sam* for his alias on that Denver trip . . . ? There was a whole other side to Butch that Sundance had never had any idea could exist.

The door opened and Butch stalked in, frowning. "I told you kids to stay *out* of here—"

" 'S okay," Sundance said. "I been sleeping too much anyway. They ain't bothering me."

Butch stood behind the boys and placed a hand on each one's shoulder. "Your ma says you've both got schoolwork to do."

"I got hardly *any*, really," Robert, Jr., protested. "Grammar's all I got to work on, and ain't nobody can't do that easy enough."

"She's really *strict*, Pa," Sam said. He did not really believe he could enlist his father against his mother in the anti-homework campaign, but you never got anywhere by not trying.

"Mothers are like that," Sundance said. "You gotta look *out* for 'em. You can't trust women to see things the way a man does . . . though that ain't to say you're not supposed to respect 'em an' obey all lawful orders accordin' to the rules an' regulations laid down. Bein' a kid's kind of like bein' an enlisted man in the army, there's a lot of bein' told what to do. Best thing is to soldier along an' make the best of it, keepin' your own opinion about the rights an' wrongs of each particular situation as it might come up."

The kids grinned, basking in the warmth of this man-to-man advice. "You ever met Butch Cassidy?" Sam asked suddenly.

"Butch . . ."

"He's an outlaw too," Bobby added excitedly. "He started out around *here*."

Sundance looked at an obviously taken-aback Butch who, after a second, gave a quick, almost imperceptible negative shake of his head.

"*Sure* I know him," Sundance said. Butch, not visible to the boys behind whom he stood, contorted his face and shook a fist at Sundance.

"What's he like?" Sam asked.

"Butch . . . well . . ." Sundance looked away from Butch, whose face was now eloquent of a yearning for a sudden murder. "He's real *short*, y'know, little bitty guy." He reached over the edge of the bed and held his hand two and a half feet above the floor to indicate just *how* little-bitty.

"And he's got these *beady* little eyes . . . sort of looks like a mole, if you've ever seen a mole. No? It's sorta like a prairie dog that's been *pulled* out, so it's got this long nose . . . uglier'n hell."

The boys' faces fell, but they nodded gravely, relegating the handsome, tall, glamorous Cassidy to the place of legend where the axe-wielding and confessionary young George Washington dwelt.

Butch glowered at Sundance and said, "C'mon, boys. He's not well yet, you can *tell* he's kinda delirious. *Go on* . . ."

The boys left reluctantly, looking back at the hero who had come to live among the fortunate Parker family. "G'night, Sundance," Sam said.

When they had gone, Butch closed the door behind them. He looked at Sundance, then went over to the window and stared at it.

"They don't know?" Sundance said after a moment.

Butch, still contemplating, without seeing, whatever might lie outside the window, shook his head. "It's the way she wants it. Me too, I guess."

Sundance looked around the room. *Their* bedroom, going by the chest of drawers and so on. Mr. and Mrs. Parker, Robert and Mary, had lived and loved here, made those kids. Now it was being used to let an on-the-run hardcase mend, while Mr. and Mrs. P. bunked down somewhere else . . . "When's the last time you saw 'em?"

"The night before I went to prison."

A last visit, courtesy of old Ray Bledsoe, yeah. Does a man some good to get known for keeping his word, he gets trusted so's he can visit his kids for a night before he gets sent up for horse stealing. His head felt tight, and he had a sudden vision of himself with a son or daughter back in Jersey, they way he'd probably have had if he'd stayed there and settled into something steady. It might have been lousy, but it'd have been hard to leave.

"Don't they ever wonder where you've been?"

Butch looked at the floor. "I've been gone more or less most of their lives. They think that's how things are." He looked at Sundance and away again, and took a long breath. "I send money."

"Sooner or later they'll find out," Sundance said.

Butch picked up the lantern the boys had left. The light, washing upward, made a stiff orange-and-black mask of his face; its expression was impossible to read. "I been thinking about that."

> Old Biff Jones had two daughters and a son,
> One went to Denver, the other went wrong.
> His wife, she died in a poolroom fight . . .

Butch supplied the words silently to try to keep the tune straight as he went through it on the harmonica, but there was no denying that there were some flats

141

and sharps getting in where they weren't supposed to be.

> *But still he keeps singin' from morning till night. . . .*

At the kitchen table where he and Bobby were attacking their schoolwork, Sam yawned and put his head down on his open book.

Mary, sitting in a straight-backed chair, mending a shirt, spoke to him warningly: "Sam . . ."

The boy lifted his head and struggled on, still yawning. Bobby, next to him, scowled. Was "running" an adverb or a predicate? No reason it *should* be a predicate, but sometimes things were when you didn't expect it, and you could get stung that way. And what was a predicate, anyway . . . ? It was *awful* late. He looked up from his work.

"You play that mouth organ good, Pa."

Butch took the harmonica from his mouth and wiped the mouthpiece. "Well, I need practice, but I got a good ear for music, they tell me," he said modestly. He ignored Mary's quirked eyebrow.

"Can you teach me?"

"Sure."

"Me, too?" Sam asked, perking up.

Butch smiled. That would be something, teaching the boys things. Harmonica, hunting, how to handle cattle—some other things he knew, no need to lumber them with those . . . A man could really feel he was a father when he was able to do that. Of course, it meant putting in time, and that wasn't easy. A straight job after being on the loose so long, that didn't come natural or pleasant, but he could stick to it, for the boys—for Mary, too. Plenty of time ahead to make up for the lost years . . .

Mary surveyed the boys and the man, the bond between them almost visible in the soft lantern light, with mixed feelings. The boys needed him . . . so did she . . . but everything was so easy and careless between them. *She* was left to do the hard things, like seeing to it they got their work done. Like now.

"Rob, their schoolwork . . ."

"They're *tired*, Mary," Butch said cajolingly. He turned to Bobby and Sam. "C'mon, boys, go to bed and you can finish that tomorrow morning."

They slammed their books shut and slid from their chairs, then made for the next room, Butch following.

"Will you play somethin' while we go to sleep, Pa?" Bobby asked.

"Sure." Butch flourished the harmonica.

Sam let out a little cheer and hugged Butch's legs as they left the room together.

Mary's fingers clenched on the mending in her lap. She looked after them, her face set and tight. The sounds of low talk and laughter, then the quavering of Butch's harmonica came to her. She winced as he hit a sour note. That was Rob—cheerful and confident of his ability to do anything, and not minding if some of the details went wrong here and there. If *she* lived like that . . . if she even did her *mending* like that . . . what would become of them?

She set her work aside, and, in a fury, went to the front room, to the cedar chest against the wall and pulled out a faded pink nightgown. Mister Robert Parker wasn't going to get the free show of her undressing that he'd enjoyed—and oh, so had she—every night since he got back. Nowhere else for him to sleep, with that friend of his in the bedroom, but Robert LeRoy Parker, Sr., could count on getting plenty of rest tonight!

When Butch came in, carrying the rolled-up mattress, he raised his eyebrows. Storm signals. Mary was in her oldest nightgown, the one that came nearest to hiding the ripeness of her body. Times past, seeing her in it, he'd known it was time to fetch out the mattress and lay it out in the front room, because there was a grandma of a fight brewing. But they were *both* sleeping in the front room now, so it looked like whatever it was was going to have to be thrashed out now.

Mary's back was eloquent with anger as she pulled two pillows from a shelf, waited with tight lips for Butch to unroll the mattress, and wordlessly tossed them onto it.

Butch sat on the mattress and began to remove his boots. He debated taking the bull by the horns—did that sound right, he wondered, since it had to do with Mary—and asking what was wrong, but came down on the negative side of the proposition. She would get to it in her own time, and why borrow trouble?

Mary pulled a quilt from the shelf. Butch stood and unbuttoned his shirt. Mary came over and stood in front of him, holding the quilt. Her face was stiff as she looked at him.

Finally she spoke. "They didn't even say goodnight to me! You snap your fingers, they run off without a backward look—never mind the work *I'll* have to make them do tomorrow!"

"They're just kids," Butch said placatingly. "They're just tired."

"*No*. They're not just kids and they weren't *that* tired." Her face held its anger-strengthened stiffness for another second, then softened into discouragement. "It's not fair."

"What's not fair?"

"That they love you more than me."

Butch relaxed a little. Not too damn much he could do with Mary when she was full of righteous wrath, but when she passed from that to feeling low and sad, *there* he could do some good. Comforting unhappy ladies came naturally to him. "They don't," he said.

In the light of the single kerosene lantern, Mary's eyes were bright with tears. "They *do*. They think I'm mean, but I'm only trying to do my best."

144

"*They* don't think that," Butch said softly, looking at her.

"Of course they do! I'm with them here and I *have* to be strict! And then you come back . . . and you win them over so *easily*! They never give me what they give you!"

She clutched the quilt to her and glared up at Butch. The tears were rolling down her cheeks now. "I thought of telling them you were *dead*, so they wouldn't get their hopes up that you'd come back. And mine."

She shook her head hopelessly and turned away from Butch. He came up behind her and slid his arms around her. His touch was gentle, but she flinched at it, then relaxed . . . just a little.

She felt the touch of his lips on her hair; in the square of mirror on the wall in front of her she could see him bent over her, see the strong arms that circled her waist, see herself in the worn nightgown . . . with the worn face about it.

"Look at us. I look so . . . old."

"No, you don't." Butch's voice was muffled by her hair. Very slowly, very gently, he drew her closer.

"I look older than you." Lantern light glowed softly on his arms.

"You *are* older than me," Butch pointed out.

"Six *months*," Mary said. After a moment she added sadly, "You'd think six years." She relaxed, almost sagged against him, now crying freely. "It's just been so *hard*, Rob!"

"I know," Butch said softly. "I know. But . . . I am back."

His arms tightened around her almost painfully; then he turned her around and kissed her. Her lips were stiff for an instant, then opened to him, and the length of her body softened and pressed itself to his.

Later, with Mary sleeping soundly—and, he estimated with some pride, contentedly—beside him,

Butch lay looking up at the dimly visible ceiling. There was a *lot* to this family life, all right. Mary, the kids . . . not exciting—well, at times, sure, like the last hour—but . . . warm.

But it took some paying for . . . and he'd better get to sleep so he'd be in shape in the morning to go on doing just that.

CHAPTER FIFTEEN

"I'll take a dozen pork chops," the woman in the tiny hat said, with the proud air of one who announces an intention to purchase a controlling interest in two major railroads.

You'd *make* a *couple* dozen pork chops, lady, Butch thought, surveying the broad face with its turned-up nose and tiny eyes, and the barrel-like body. He speculated for a moment on how she would butcher up and dress out, and thought wistfully that it might be fun to try. You met all sorts in this job, most of them worse than the rest, it seemed to him, which didn't make sense, but got the feeling about right. But it was no business of his if the pig-lady wanted to commit cannibalism. He was there to serve her, to *serve* the horde of meat-hungry customers waiting impatiently behind her, to *serve* old Skinner, the owner, by making money for him, which he was constantly hovering behind Butch to see that he damn well *did*. . . . "Yes, ma'am."

He ripped a piece of butcher paper off the roll next to him, laid it on the block, slapped a meaty loin onto it, and with the cleaver deftly sliced off twelve chops. *Yes, ma'am.* That Deadwood Dick fellow, now, spending his days saying "Yes, sir" and "Yes, ma'am" and shining folks' shoes and making their beds and fetching them drinks and brushing them off . . . That had struck Butch as a way of living that would be pretty hard to take.

And here he was, yes-sirring and yes-ma'aming to beat the band. . . . At least old Deadwood got to wear a snappy blue uniform, not a beat-up straw hat and bloody apron. . . .

"Too much *paper*, Parker." Skinner's flinty voice reproved him from behind. "That stuff costs good money, y'know."

"Yessir," Butch mumbled. Why don't he buy some costs *bad* money, then . . . ?

A thin woman with angry ice-blue eyes of the kind that Butch had previously seen only on the most deranged and murderous gunfighters evidently decided she had been waiting long enough, and screamed from behind the fat woman, "Gimme six pounds of beefsteak!"

"Be with you in a *minute*, ma'am," Butch said, hurriedly starting to wrap the chops. I'll throw the meat right into your cage soon's I can.

"Trim the *fat*," the large lady said, looking at him coldly. "I'm not payin' for *fat*. Trim it offa them *chops*."

Right, lady. Why pay for fat? You got a lifetime supply already. Butch took a deep breath, nodded, and grabbed a thin-bladed knife from the rack. He sliced the white fat away from the edges of the chops, scooting it into the scrap barrel with the knife. One thing, he could do this stuff with some skill, and that was in its own way kind of satisfying—

"*Closer*," the fat woman grunted.

"Right." Using the knife almost as a razor now, he shaved a few remnants of fat from the edge of one chop and started on another.

"What are you *doing*, Parker?"

Its wielder's concentration broken, the knife slid easily from the chop into Butch's forefinger. Blood welled up instantly, and Butch stuck the finger in his mouth. Around it, he said, with some loss of clarity, "She asked me to trim the fat."

148

Skinner looked at the fat woman coldly. "Tell her to go somewhere else if she don't like the fat."

"There *isn't* any place else," Butch mumbled, still sucking on the finger.

"*Now* you got it," Skinner said with sour satisfaction. "And stop bleeding on the meat!"

Noon finally came, as it always did, though some days it seemed unlikely that Butch could make it that far, and he was released for the half-hour Skinner reluctantly allowed him for lunch. "Ever'body's goin' soft now," he had complained. "The ten-hour day, and I don't know what all. *Lunch* hours. When I come out here, men in trade put in *time*. They et on the job, a sandwich or as it might be a chicken leg in one hand whiles as they waited on the customer. When I started up, *I* didn't take no time for such stuff as lunchin'. Meat was my life. I lived meat, sold meat, slept meat, I *was* meat."

Recalling this conversation as he walked quickly to the lunch counter he favored, Butch mentally consigned a neatly trimmed side of Skinner to a meat hook alongside this morning's fat lady.

Circleville was really coming on, growing and changing a good bit since he was last there. A soda fountain, complete with young fellows in pinch-waisted suits leaning against its front and ogling whatever girls might pass; overhead wires for the telephone system; two phonograph stores, one featuring the old reliable Edison cylinder machines, the other pushing the new disc-shaped records; a barber shop advertising a lady barber . . . might be interesting, Mary could hardly object if a man felt like keeping himself spruce and businesslike. . . .

But a lot of the old Circleville remained: the plank sidewalks, the hitching posts, farm wagons drawn up in front of various stores. Further down the street, the U.S. Marshal's office, much the same as it had been in the past. Fortunately, Butch's limited excursions into town didn't take him past there. Nobody in Utah wanted him urgently right now, but there were probably some old posters and such around there, and he didn't want anybody making a connection between Butch Cassidy and Parker, Skinner's soft-spoken assistant. Circleville was tame enough now so that the old dodderer they had for a marshal wasn't looking for trouble, anyhow. From the little Butch had heard, he had his hand full pacifying the local ranchers about the losses they were suffering from rustlers.

He ducked into the lunch counter and took a stool.

"A nice piece a' steak, Mr. Parker?" the counterman asked. "Or a porkchop, fried potatoes? We got *good* pork chops today."

Butch shook his head. "Fried egg, some beans." After a morning at Skinner's, meat was the last thing that could tempt his appetite.

"Okay, the usual," the counterman said dispiritedly.

Butch fished a notebook out of his trousers, set it on the counter, and began jotting down figures and making calculations. Groceries and truck, so much—that item was a little less than it might have been, Skinner being prepared to take half-price on Saturday for meat that wouldn't keep till Monday; clothes and staples, so much; feed for the horses, so much. He sighed. They could keep going, but it didn't look as if there was much prospect of getting any ahead. If he were to do a little more figuring, it might . . . He grimaced and slapped the notebook shut. They could wait for another time. A man might as well relax on his lunch hour—*half*-hour. He slid from the stool and fetched a copy of the *Salt Lake Herald* from a pile on a table against the wall. Circleville, a town with a strong Mormon element, tended to frown on gambling, and reading the newspaper at lunch was one of the few approved activities with some sporting element attached to it. The understood rule was that a patron was allowed to read the paper free of charge, so long as he returned it to the pile in pristine, and salable, condition. Food stains or crumpling or any rips meant that the paper had to be purchased. With a fried egg and beans facing him, Butch estimated that the odds were too severe to be worth going against, and dropped his two cents in the box next to the journals.

"Here y'*are*," the counterman said, sliding the plate of food into position before Butch, deftly making sure that the lower edge of the newspaper dripped into the juicy beans.

"Don't bother," Butch said, looking up from the headlines. "I already bought it."

"Oh. Anything interestin' in the *Herald* this time?"

"Not much," Butch said grimly, holding the paper in front of him. "Some old-time badman jailed over in Wyoming." He dug into his egg and mixed the yolk with the beans.

"Kind of a dyin' breed," the counterman observed. "All seem to be gettin' killed or gettin' chased out. Place'll be safe for decent folks like you an' me in not too long."

"Expect so."

"Anything in there about the new marshal? They retired ol' Ponder, got some new fellow in, I hear. But I don't s'pose a big old Salt Lake newspaper's gonna pay much attention to doin's in Circleville."

"Expect not."

The counterman sighed, and drifted away. That Parker kept to himself, all right, never willing to settle into a good jawing session about local happenings. Couldn't get much out of him, couldn't pass on much to him. Seemed as if he wanted as little as possible to do with Circleville. And if that was so, what was he doing here?

Butch, reading and rereading the news story on the front page of the *Herald*, was asking himself much the same thing.

* * *

151

Sundance gritted his teeth as he reached up to the cottonwood limb and slung the string over it. He knotted it and let the bottle fastened to its other end dangle two feet below the limb.

He took a few deep breaths, then tied two other bottles to the branch.

"Looks like it's hard for him," Sam observed from where he and Bobby lay hidden in the branches of a nearby tree.

"A gut shot, it takes some while to git better from that," Bobby said knowledgeably. "No bones broke, but a lot of muscles an' stuff tore up."

"It'd hurt to git shot in the guts, wouldn't it?" Sam said thoughtfully.

"*Sure,*" his brother replied. "But outlaws don't worry about gittin' hurt."

Sundance stepped stiffly away from the tree. Each step, though light, jolted his belly with pain, and it helped to time his breathing to his walk.

Twenty paces away, he turned and faced the dangling bottles. His right hand streaked for the gun at his side, but stopped short of it as fire ran through his midsection.

He compressed his lips, bent slightly at the knees, and poised his hand over the gun butt. The boys waited expectantly.

They saw only a flicker of the hand, then the pistol was out of the holster and firing—faster, it seemed to them, than they'd ever been able to rattle a stick along a picket fence.

The leftmost bottle, its supporting string severed, began to drop to the ground, but exploded in midair as a slug tore through it. So did the second. The third bottle, however, touched the ground an instant before the last shot shattered it.

The boys looked on, awed.

Sundance shook his head in disgust. "Slow . . . too slow . . ." he muttered. He made his way painfully back to the tree and bent to select three more bottles from the pile next to it.

The youthful face contorted in a terrible grimace of pain and gave out a cry indicative of a fatal wound. Its owner clutched his stomach, staggered, lurched in a half-circle and plunged to the ground, to lie face up with open eyes staring into the twilight sky and into the somber face of the one who had brought him to this dire moment.

Sam looked up and said, "It's *my* turn to be Sundance now."

Bobby shoved the bent stick which he had whittled into something like a pistol into his belt. "Uh-*uh*. You're still Cassidy."

Sam sat up indignantly. "I don't want to be Cassidy anymore! He's an ugly little runt!"

"So? *You're* an ugly little runt."

Sam stormed toward his brother, arms flailing. Bobby laughed and easily sidestepped him. Sam's roundhouse swings hit only empty air, bringing the younger boy to a new peak of impotent fury. He stopped swinging, took a deep, sobbing breath, and began to cry.

"Bob*by*!" his mother's voice called from the kitchen window. "Let Sam be Sundance for a while. You be Cassidy."

"I don't want to be Cassidy!" Bobby protested. Sam knuckled a tear-stained face, a smirk beginning to replace the scowl. Bobby could push him around easy enough, but Ma, she had no trouble at *all* making Bobby toe the line. Now *he* knew how it felt. He wondered if anyone pushed Ma around. Pa, maybe . . . ?

In the kitchen, Butch, his shirt off and suspenders dangling, stopped sponging his chest to say, "That's a hell of a note. My own kids . . ."

They heard Bobby's renewed complaint from outside:

"Cassidy don't do nothin' good!"

"Cassidy *doesn't* do anything *well*," Mary called, in a reflexive correction of the grammar, if not the sentiment. She turned to Butch and smiled at his irritated countenance. "Obviously, they've never seen him bed."

She was not used to finding herself saying such things and a red tinge spread over her face. But . . . here in the kitchen, the heart of her house, making dinner for her menfolk, her man standing there half-naked and smoothly clean—and the new clothes washer he'd bought with his first week's pay standing in the corner like a solid commitment that said he'd go *on* being there—there was no denying that it all came together to make her feel safe, wanted, and excited all at once, and no harm in an old married lady who felt like that talking a little frisky.

"Is that any way for a nice Mormon girl to talk?" Butch said, taking a half-step toward her.

Mary met his gaze boldly, then glanced deliberately down his body and took a shallow breath. "Whoever said I was that nice?"

"*Well.*" Butch looked at her with renewed interest. "Isn't that . . . uh . . . nice?" He was very close to her now, and took a strand of hair that had fallen onto her forehead and gently stroked it. She drew his hand down and brushed it with open, moist lips, then turned her face hungrily up to his.

His arms went tightly around her, and he could feel a heavy, urgent heartbeat—his, hers, he couldn't be sure—where their bodies joined. Her fingertips moved on his back, kneading, pressing, nails digging. . . .

"Ma!" Sam yelled. "Bobby says he won't *play* if he's gotta be Cassidy!"

Butch lifted his face from Mary's. "What's Sundance been *telling* them?" he demanded plaintively.

Mary stepped back and straightened her hair. "I'll get on with dinner. If you're so interested in that, you could ask him."

154

Butch did not need to ask: Sundance supplied the answer copiously at the dinner table, with wild fables of his luckless association with the inept Cassidy.

The boys were spellbound, and paid hardly any attention to their supper. Mary, finishing early, escaped the full force of his imaginative reminiscence by going to the washing machine and cranking a load of clothes through it. Butch, bone-tired after another endless day at Skinner's, picked at his food and listened glumly.

". . . so then I said, 'Butch, if you put the dynamite on *top* of the safe, why, you just got to know that won't open it. But you know ol' Butch, stubborn as a mule an' twice as ugly—"

"I don't know how you ever put *up* with him," Butch said, with a sour glance at his sons' shining faces.

"—he puts the stuff on top and lights it and there's this huge explosion and when the smoke clears we see the safe has gone right through the floor of the train an' lodged between the tracks." He grinned and shook his head at the sublime stupidity of Butch Cassidy.

"So then what did you do, Sundance?" Sam asked eagerly.

"Yeah, what *did* you do, Sundance?" Butch asked, relishing the chance to put his traducer in an awkward spot. "I mean, you were so much *smarter* than Butch, how'd you figure out how to get the money out of the safe after dumb old Butch had messed things up?"

"What?" Sundance said, sensing the trap.

"You *did* get the money, didn't you?"

Sundance glanced uneasily at the boys' worshipful eyes. "Sure."

Butch's "*How?*" was triumphant and remorseless. He smiled at Sundance, enjoying the answering glare.

"Well . . . see . . . uh . . ." Sudden inspiration struck him. His eyes brightened and he leaned toward the boys. "What I didn't tell you was that the train was on a bridge at the time—"

"A bridge?" Butch cut in "You stopped a train on a *bridge* to rob it?"

Sundance nodded and gave him the grave, condescending smile of the expert explaining his craft to the uninformed. "It's the *perfect* place." Before Butch could react, he turned to the boys and went on, "So even though the safe was wedged between the tracks, it was hanging down under the bridge, so all I had to do was have Butch hold me by the feet while I hung upside down and cleaned it out."

The boys looked at him with slack-jawed admiration.

"It's a wonder," Butch said bitterly, "he didn't drop you on your head."

Mary pulled the wash from the machine's wooden tub, dumped it into a copper boiler to rinse, and came over to the table. She lifted the plates from in front of her sons' places and said briskly, "All right, boys. Time for your schoolwork. *Go* on."

Sam and Bobby grumbled, but slid from their chairs and made for the other room.

"Why are you trying to make me look bad?" Sundance said in an angry whisper.

Butch gave him an incredulous look. "I'm trying to make *you* look bad? What're you doing to *me*?"

Sundance looked defiantly at him. "They want to hear stories, and I'm all out of my own."

"*Yeah*," Butch said angrily. "Well, don't take what happened to me and say it happened to you. You take every dumb thing Elza Lay or Flat Nose George or them ever done and write it up to *my* account. You're giving my boys some fun and making yourself a big man with 'em. But the way it's working out is, they think Butch Cassidy is a horse's ass!"

The two men glared at each other, then Sundance stood up and shoved his chair back. The movement, and the raw tension between them, reminded both for a second of the moment back in the cabin in Brown's Hole last fall, just before their partnership had been settled.

Sundance's eyes flickered briefly around the orderly kitchen, took in Mary, standing with a worried look by the sink, and the room in which Butch's—Robert Parker's—sons were studying. It was great, but no place for him. Not for Butch Cassidy, either. Robert Parker, yes—and Butch better get it straight in his head *soon* whether he was Parker or Cassidy. . . .

After a few seconds he delivered a slow, icy reply to Butch's complaint. "Maybe he is." He turned and slammed out of the door.

Butch slammed his fist onto the table and let out an exasperated explosion of breath.

Mary came over to him. "What's the matter with you?" she asked, resting a hand on his shoulder. "You don't usually mind Sundance having a little fun, even when he gets rough about it."

"I don't know . . ." Butch sighed and looked up at her. "Yes, I do. In town today I read in the paper that Mike Cassidy is in jail in Wyoming. Gonna go on trial soon."

Mary looked at him with concern. She knew what Mike Cassidy had meant to young Robert Parker—so much that he had adopted the older man's name when he hit the outlaw trail. She shook her head and returned to her task of scraping the supper plates.

A clatter of hoofs told them that Sundance had gone off on one of the aimless night rides he claimed he needed to get back into shape. When the sound had died away, Mary spoke up tentatively. "Rob?"

Butch looked up at her distractedly, as if he had been suddenly called back from a mental journey to a place a long way off.

"You're not . . . going to try anything? Like trying to spring Mike out of jail or something?"

Butch's "no" came just too late to be completely convincing. He went on, "But poor old Mike . . ."

Mary sat in the chair across from him, leaned across the table, and spoke with quiet urgency. "Let his being in jail make you realize that what you're doing right here, right now, is *right*. Be glad it's not *you* in there. It could have been—and there's always the chance that it could be, even if you don't do anything more; you're still wanted in some places—"

"I *explained* about that," Butch said. "Things die down, after a while nobody's gonna bother following 'em up. Not a chance in a hundred any of that old stuff'll ever—"

"Even a chance in a *hundred* is enough to make me come awake at night when I hear a sound that makes me think maybe they've come for you! There's something other women have that I don't—that chance in a hundred takes it away from me. All right, I'll pay that price to have you back, and I'm willing to pay it, Rob Parker." She stopped and looked at him, her face full of love . . . and warning. "But that's top dollar. We're together, and we're going to go on being together, and you *know* just how much I can make that worth your while, mister—"

Butch grinned appreciatively.

"—but I can only do that for Rob Parker. Butch Cassidy doesn't live here anymore."

Butch nodded slowly, and her face softened. "I know this has been hard for you these past weeks. . . ."

Butch pushed his chair back from the table and stood up. "*I'll* be okay . . . after Sundance is strong enough to leave. He's . . . restless, and it's making me that way." He gave her a forced smile.

She looked at him gravely, then turned again to the dishes. She took comfort in scrubbing them clean, rinsing them, drying them, stacking them ready for the next meal and the meals after that. A clean dish was a

158

clean dish, something you could make sure of, all it needed was the knowledge of what you wanted and the will to see to the task.

But a man wasn't like that. . . .

CHAPTER SIXTEEN

Butch grunted as he hoisted the heavy side of beef high enough to catch on the hook that would display it in the front window. The meaty smell enveloped him, and the heft of his burden and the close embrace of it his task called for were horribly reminiscent of the way he had held Mary close last night, when she cried in her sleep. I do this much longer, he thought, I won't be able to see anybody as anything except walking meat.

The side of beef was in place now, and he looked past it at the three customers waiting outside the still-closed store. Yesterday's fat lady, same hat. Probably went through the dozen chops at a sitting last night, coming back for more. A pinch-faced young girl in a shabby dress: "Ma wants ten cents' worth of round steak for the dog, please"—that'd be her order. If Skinner was anything like a safe distance away, Butch could slice out a remarkably hefty dime portion, knowing that it was what the kid and her Ma would live on for the day. And a man in work clothes, looking mad. Butch sized him up as having quarreled with his wife, so no lovingly prepared lunch to take with him on the job: four slices bologna sausage, maybe head cheese, and the next stop the bakery down the street for a fresh roll to eat it on, come noon.

He closed his eyes. Robert LeRoy Parker, you are getting to know more about the meat trade than anyone ought to.

"Hurry *up*, Parker, we gotta open up." Skinner's tone was comparatively mild, no worse than running your fingernail across a slate; he was in his element, turning a carcass into steaks, roasts, chops, and salable scraps with loving artistry. Butch knew that Skinner had already given himself his day's treat, the dressing of two elegant crown roasts of lamb, alone in the back room, and was thankful that he had not seen his boss's expression while engaged in this rite.

He nodded, caught hold of another side of beef, trotted it to the window and thrust it up toward the one vacant hook. It caught on the first try, and he was about to step away from it when he stopped dead in shock.

O.C. Hanks was eight feet away, riding slowly by, and not looking—yet—toward him. Butch ducked behind the dangling side of beef, then cursed as he saw that the sudden movement had attracted Hanks's attention.

After a moment he peered out from behind the meat, careful not to let his face be seen. Hanks paused, then kneed his horse into a slow amble, splashing ahead, through the puddles last night's rain had left in the street.

Skinner's voice came from the back room—probably gloating over his crown roasts for an extra few minutes before offering them up for sale, Butch thought: "Two minutes to opening time, Parker. You see to it to the second, hear?"

"Yes*sir!*" Butch called. As he spoke, he was stripping off his apron, rolling it and his straw hat into an untidy bundle, and grabbing his street jacket and hat and getting into them.

"Right away, sir!" He unlatched the front door and opened it, stepping outside to where the prospective customers waited.

"You open, Mister?" the fat woman said. "I want—"

Butch shook his head. "Been closed down by the

sanitary inspector," he said. "Wouldn't *believe* what they found in there, didn't know it myself, bein' only out front. I'm *shaken,* lady, deeply shaken. Don't know as I'll ever eat meat again."

The fat woman and the workman retreated hastily. The girl started to drift off down the street. "Here," Butch said. "Ain't you Delores Higgins?"

"No, I'm Ada Bender."

Butch snapped his fingers. "*That* was the name I was lookin' for, on the tip of my tongue all the time. Your ma sent you down for some meat for the dog, right?"

"The . . . cat," the girl said, looking at her shoe tops. "But now the store's been—"

"Well, here, now." Butch slid a greenback into her hand. "I feel kind of responsible, though bein' only a employee, and I think you ought to take this an' get that cat a steak or a pork chop or such at the lunch counter there an' take it home to him. *Least* I can do. Get on, now."

He sent her on her way, then ran to where his horse was hitched.

Mary looked at him, her lips tight. From the instant she had heard the hoofbeats of his returning horse, at this early hour of the day, she had known that what she had most feared had in some way come about. His silent, efficient packing of travel gear and supplies into his saddlebags only confirmed that.

"I have to clear out of here for a while," Butch said.

"Why?" She had to ask the question, though the answer did not really interest her. The fact was what mattered, not the reason.

"Because somebody who wants to kill me is in town." Butch jammed a wool shirt into the bag, and was about to do the same with his harmonica; instead he stuck it into the pocket of his coat.

162

"Does he know you're here?"

"Not yet, but he will." He looked at her earnestly. "If I leave now, he'll follow me. That way he can't do any harm to you and the boys."

Mary closed her eyes. There *would* be something to this nightmare that showed it was all for her own good, wouldn't there? At least the way Robert Butch Parker Cassidy would put it . . . "Then . . . after he leaves?"

"I'll wait a while, let things simmer down a bit . . . then come back."

She looked at him disconsolately. "It's all going to start again, isn't it?"

"It's *not* going to start again!" Butch frowned impatiently as he slid his revolver into the saddlebag.

"Then why are you taking that?" Her tone was black.

"Because . . . because you don't go out there without one." He looked at her quickly. "Where are the boys? I want to tell them good-bye."

Distantly, Mary said, "They're with Sundance. At the creek."

He nodded and picked up the saddlebags. Mary followed him outside. He threw the bags over his already-saddled horse, then turned to her. He held her, but only lightly, feeling the stiffness of her body.

"I'll be *back*," he said.

She shook her head violently; tears spilled onto her cheeks.

"I *promise* I will."

She let out a long-held breath. "I won't be here. I . . . won't wait for you again." It was a statement, forlorn and accepting, not a complaint or threat.

"Mary, *I* couldn't help O.C. showing up."

She nodded. "I know. It's not your fault, it's just how things are . . . *who* you are. Something . . . always . . . happens."

Mary looked up at him and stepped back; his arms fell away from her. Her face was older-looking than it had been, and harder, but composed.

"Good-bye, Robert."

She turned and entered the cabin. Butch watched the door close, silently but firmly, behind her.

He looked at the cabin for a moment. There was no movement at either of the windows facing him. The cabin was closed in on itself, shut against him. He looked beyond it, to the peaks that lay to the east, then in sudden haste mounted his horse and rode away, not looking back.

The rock-strewn creek where the boys loved to fish was just out of sight of the cabin. He found them there with Sundance—whose horse, he was glad to see, was tethered to a nearby tree.

"How's the fishing?" he called, as he dismounted.

Sam trotted over to him, uncurious about his presence during a work day, only pleased. "Want to try?" He held up his crudely whittled pole and line.

"I'd like to, Sam," Butch said, looking down at him, "but . . . I can't. I've got to go."

Sundance looked at him closely and raised his eyebrows. Butch gave a quick nod. "I'm gonna have to be away for a while."

"*Why?*" Bobby said.

"Something came up." He looked at Sundance, who returned his nod almost imperceptibly.

"I don't *want* you to go," Sam wailed, and looked away.

Butch reached down toward his head, almost touched it, and halted the gesture.

Sam, fighting back tears, looked up at him again. "Is Sundance going, too?"

Sundance spoke up gently. "Yes. We both have to go."

Bobby nodded three times, very slowly, looking down at the ground.

Butch cleared his throat and said, "Try not to fight too much. Okay?"

Sam said, "Okay." Bobby was silent.

Butch reached into his pocket and pulled out the battered harmonica. He held it down to Sam. "Here, take care of this for me."

The boy's eyes lit up. "Really?"

Butch nodded. "Let Bobby use it, too." Bobby looked up, some of his sullenness evaporating in a new interest. "See if you can learn to play something for me . . . by the time I get back."

He stopped. There seemed to be nothing more to say to his sons. He was going, he'd be back, don't fight. . . . Mind your Ma? Hell, they'd do *that* without any telling from him. There should be something else, but, if there was, it didn't come easily to mind. . . .

"You guys stay here and catch some big ones, okay?" Sundance said. The boys nodded, their mood lightening. This was an awful moment, but you had awful moments, and came through them. There was still some good fishing today, and the fascinating business of trying out the mysterious harmonica.

As Butch and Sundance walked toward their horses, they could hear the beginnings of a quarrel over who was to have first whack at it.

"I'll go back to the house and get my stuff," Sundance told Butch.

"I brought it."

Sundance watched Butch swing into the saddle, then glanced back at the boys. They had dropped the harmonica controversy and were baiting their hooks. He walked back to them and crouched next to where they sat on the creek bank.

He checked to see that Butch was out of earshot, and spoke quietly to them. "Listen, what I said about Butch Cassidy?"

They looked up at him. Dirt tracks from the tears were barely dry on Sam's face, but his and Bobby's expressions were mainly of polite interest. Their father, and Sundance, who had flashed across their skies like a comet, were going away, so what Sundance might have to say already belonged to the past.

"That he was just an ugly little mole? Well, it's not true. He's actually a fairly nice-looking fella . . . and kind of smarter than I said." He gave a brief flick of a backward glance toward Butch, mounted and impatient. "And not the worst guy I ever met. Okay?"

They nodded, their eyes drifting toward their baited hooks and the rushing stream.

"I just wanted you to know that," Sundance said. He rose to his feet and walked toward where Butch waited.

CHAPTER SEVENTEEN

Sundance waited until the trail along the creek took them out of sight of the boys before speaking. "Nice weather for riding. That rain last night kind of makes everything fresh-smelling."

Butch said nothing.

"Something came up, I think you said. What *kinda* something? Old warrant drifted in, a something like that? Or did you finally get it sorted out you was Butch Cassidy an' not Robert LeRoy Parker? Shame you hadda put them boys an' that woman through it again before you made up your mind, but—"

"Lay *off* that, Sundance!" Butch said savagely. "When this is . . . when I can, I'll get back to them."

Sundance glanced sideways at him. "Sure."

Butch looked at the trail ahead and said, "See, I got to move on for a little, till things blow over, and seeing as you're pretty near mended, seemed like it'd be good for us to travel on a ways together. . . ."

"Things blow over." Sundance turned the phrase over in his mind for a moment, then asked, "What things?"

"Man come into town, I saw him this morning at the store. Fellow who's gunning for me."

"For Cassidy, not Parker? I don't s'pose as it's someone you give short weight or sold spoiled beef to?"

Butch nodded.

"Why don't you just face this guy?"

Butch warmed a little to the familiar chore of laying

out the logic of a situation. "Because if I kill him I'll be right back where I started. But he's a better shot than me and he'll probably kill me."

"Then your troubles are over," Sundance pointed out.

"Terrific."

They jogged along for a few moments, angling away from the creek, as Butch checked his memory for a stopping place for the night. A boardinghouse or such in Antimony would be comfortable, but it might be more sensible just to camp out, maybe somewhere along the Otter.

"Who is he?"

"Who is who?"

"This fellow who's gunning for you and making us light out for parts unknown, at least to me, *that's* who. I'd kind of like to know in case I run into him some time an' want to thank him for the interesting excursion."

Butch shrugged.

"I don't think I heard you," Sundance said acidly.

It took him a couple of seconds to register and interpret Butch's mumbled answer: ". . . nks . . ."

"Hanks?" He reined up his horse. "The sonofabitch who shot *me*?"

Butch gave a reluctant half-nod, then spoke quickly: "Yeah, but listen—he wasn't *aiming* at you, Sundance, it was me he was shooting at."

"Oh, *well!*" Sundance snarled. "Then that makes it all right!" He half stood in his stirrups and shouted at Butch, "He almost killed me!"

He pulled his horse up short, reined it around, and started back down the trail at a gallop. Butch sighed and rode after him.

When Butch caught up, he called, "Sundance!"

Sundance slowed to a trot and looked sharply at him. "You been thinking up any more arguments about forgive and forget? Lemme tell you . . ."

Butch shook his head. "Just . . . there's a fork of the trail that bypasses the cabin. Let's take that, huh? Feel sort of strange, Mary and the kids seeing us ride by again just after we left."

Sundance nodded. Feel even stranger, wouldn't it, *you* seeing *them?* Once a man's said that hard a good-bye, it don't do to remind himself about it too much.

They got to Circleville a lot quicker, Butch reflected gloomily, than he'd made it just that morning, or most mornings on the way to work at Skinner's. It made a difference when the traveler was looking forward to something pleasurable and interesting, the way Sundance was to the prospect of killing someone or getting killed.

He glanced at Skinner's shop nervously as they passed. It was closed, a hastily lettered sign in the window saying it was on account of illness. Had Skinner somehow taken that about the sanitary inspector seriously? Or had he gone fighting crazy when he'd heard about it and had to be locked up? Something he'd never know . . . until he got back, of course.

"We better, uh, find some place we can ask around on the quiet," Butch said. "Some saloon or so where likely we'd get word about O.C. In case he ain't already gone, just passing through, like," he added hopefully. A good, sound plan had just come to him with the vividness of a scene in a stage play: a bar, him conversing with some tough-looking character, well away from Sundance, about the crops or anything else, coming back to report reluctantly that someone answering O.C.'s description had been seen riding out for Salt Lake some hours ago. Would Sundance buy that? Maybe yes, maybe no. But worth a try . . .

"What kind of horse this Hanks riding?" Sundance asked abruptly.

"Mean-looking roan, ain't been curried in a long time," Butch answered automatically, then cursed himself.

Sundance scanned the street ahead. "Like that one?" He pointed at a horse cumbered with greasy saddlebags tethered outside the barber shop.

"Some."

"It *is* that one, ain't it?" Sundance said sharply.

"It could be . . . yeah."

Sundance headed his horse for the nearest hitching post, swung off it, and slipped the reins over the post; Butch slowly followed his example.

Here's O.C. Hanks, he thought bitterly, known far and wide as a man that don't observe the rule that cleanliness is next to godliness any more than a polecat does, and the first thing he does when he hits a town is go and get himself shaved and trimmed, or whatever. It was awful hard to make good plans when people kept doing dumb things. He glanced at the shop and saw again the sign advertising the services of a lady barber. Probably pining for female companionship, after so long away from Emma, Butch decided. The barbering, the woman, and what O.C. was about to come up against reminded Butch of that Samson, in the Bible, only the elements of the story seemed a little jumbled.

Sundance had his pistol out, the cylinder flipped to one side, and was dropping cartridges into each chamber after inspecting them minutely. One failed to meet his approval, and he tossed it into a puddle in the muddy street.

Butch shook his head. Last night, he'd heard the rain drumming on the cabin roof as he'd held Mary. Now Mary was a long way away, somewhere on the other side of a door he'd passed through, as if last night were years ago. But the street was still mired from that same rain, and rings were spreading in a puddle of it from Sundance's discarded bullet. . . .

"You're not a hundred percent yet," he told Sundance.

"He doesn't know that." Sundance dropped another load into the gun.

"I mean, if you're just a fraction of a second late—"

"I won't be."

"You can't be *sure* of that."

Sundance glared at him. "I been practicing!"

"Shooting bottles," Butch said. "Bottles don't shoot *back.*"

Sundance sighted down the loaded gun, spun the cylinder, and flipped it into his holster. "Tell him I'm out here," he said flatly.

Butch shook his head. "No, I—"

"Then I'm goin' in." Sundance started toward the shop door.

Butch quickly stepped into his path and said hotly, "Okay, okay! I'll tell him."

Sundance relaxed, then tensed again as Butch, instead of heading for the street door to the barber shop, made for the alley beside the building. "Where you going?"

"I'm doing this, I'll do it my way," Butch said. Sundance looked after him dubiously. Butch had a way of dressing up simple things until you wouldn't recognize them, it seemed to him. By the time Butch got halfway started at something, anybody else'd have it over and done with.

He noticed with irritation that passersby were slowing to look at him as he stood on the plankwalk, then hurrying on as they caught his glance. We don't get on with this, he thought, everybody'll see there's something in the air and be crowding around to see the fun.

At the rear of the barber shop, Butch eased the door open and slipped inside. He was in a small storage room lined with shelves on which stood bottles and cardboard boxes with floridly colored labels. Inspecting one of those, he wondered briefly just what it did

171

for a Utah farmer or cowhand to have his scalp doused with stuff that smelled like whorehouse perfume and was guaranteed to have won three gold medals at international expositions.

There was a curtain covering the doorway in front of him. He parted it slightly and peered into the main room of the shop.

O.C. Hanks, a sheet tied around his neck, sat in a plain wooden chair with his head thrown back and his eyes closed. A slab-faced woman cut along the general lines of O.C., but scaled down a little—Butch wondered briefly how many customers attracted by the allurement of being handled by a lady barber ever came back for repeat business—was halfway through removing the stubble from his broad face with a gleaming straight razor.

Butch eased back the hammer on his drawn pistol and stepped through the curtain as the woman turned away from Hanks to rinse the razor in a basin of water that stood on a shelf behind her.

Seeing Butch, she stopped, her eyes going wide. He drew a finger across his lips, underscoring the gesture with a wave of his gun. She raised her eyebrows, then nodded. He pointed at the razor she held, and extended his hand. She laid the handle in his palm.

He reholstered his gun, tiptoed over to where Hanks sat patiently waiting for the resumption of his shave, and laid the blade gently alongside Hanks's Adam's apple.

"Now listen, O.C.," Butch said softly, leaning down to him, "I don't want any trouble."

Hanks's startled jump, though slight, was enough to send beads of blood welling from a thin line on his throat. He ignored the sting, and asked hoarsely, "What'd you say?"

Butch shook his head at his forgetfulness, and addressed himself to Hanks's good ear. "I said I don't want any trouble."

Hanks swiveled his head around, heedless of the razor at his neck, and gave him a contemptuous look. "This your new style, Butch—gettin' people from behind?"

"I'm trying to save your life," Butch said urgently.

Hanks rolled his eyes down toward the gleaming blade held just under his chin. "By cuttin' my throat?"

"*Listen*," Butch said, "I know I can't convince you I didn't lead Bledsoe to you . . . *can* I?"

Hanks shook his head.

"*Okay*. Look, I could slit you from ear to ear, but I've never killed anybody and I don't plan to start now. I'm not gonna fight you, but there's somebody outside right now who will—"

"Who?" Hanks asked with some interest. There was enough strange stuff in this business already, what with the man he was after holding a razor on him but seemingly inclined to talk rather than act, and now something *else* new. A man got involved with Butch Cassidy, he could count on surprises.

"The Sundance Kid."

Hanks pondered this a moment, then shook his head. "I don't have no beef with nobody called that."

"Well, he wants you. When you tried to bushwhack me back in Horse Canyon, you hit him. And he doesn't have a forgiving nature. So if I were you, I'd get out that back door, get on my horse, and get the hell out of here."

"You're bluffin'," Hanks said. "They ain't nobody out there." He smirked. Butch wasn't going to weasel out of this one.

"There is," Butch said earnestly. "And believe me, O.C., he's the best I ever saw." Hanks was clearly unconvinced, but Butch persisted. "Better than . . . Doc Holliday."

"Now, don't think—"

"Hanks?" Sundance's impatient voice came from outside. "Come on out, you yellow bastard!"

173

Butch took advantage of Hanks's momentary consternation to urge him, "Go on, O.C.—go on out the back and I'll stall him till you get away."

Hanks shook his head. "Man wants to fight, O.C. Hanks don't back away." His hand was raised to untie the sheet from around his neck when Sundance appeared in the doorway, hand poised above his gun. Butch sighed and lifted the razor away from Hanks's throat. Might have been best to cut him a *little*, accidental-like, enough to slow him down and remove him temporarily from the fighting category, but it was too late for that now.

"You want to come out?" Sundance snarled. "Or do you want to do this in here?" The woman barber shuddered and closed her eyes. The place wasn't much, but there would be even less of it after an exchange of gunfire. A couple of wild shots into the bottles in the supply room would come close to wiping her out.

Hanks whipped the sheet from around his neck and pushed himself out of the chair. "I'm comin' out."

He started for the door, then turned to face Butch. "When I'm finished with him . . ." he rumbled, "*you.*"

"Uh . . ." Butch said, and ran his fingers over his left cheek. Hanks scowled, grabbed the sheet again, and wiped the drying lather from the unshaved side of his face.

Sundance stepped from the plankwalk into a puddle in the street as Hanks emerged from the shop. Mean-looking cuss, Sundance decided. Big, too, but probably fast and light on his feet for all that bulk. Gun slung low from the waist, just where that beefy hand could drop it easily, no fancy swivel holster or anything tricky, just a working gunman's first-class equipment. No pushover.

The cool rage he depended on in a shooting scrape seeped through him, making every detail of what he

174

saw clear, but focusing on the significant things only. Butch, now coming out of the shop behind Hanks and looking worried as a mother hen, was an irrelevant detail. Hanks, the way he held himself and moved, the way he'd be thinking . . . those were what mattered. A twinge of pain from his belly sharpened the rage.

Another detail fed itself into his calculations. At the corner of his vision, he could see a stir, the beginnings of a gathering crowd. Kids, loafers, drifting up. He'd have to work it so they'd be firing down the street, not chancing a stray shot going into the crowd. That happened, it'd be necktie party for whoever was still around when the gunplay stopped.

"I heard you got a complaint," Hanks called.

"I don't like people going around putting holes in me."

Hanks grinned and stepped from the plankwalk into the mud of the street. "How long's that been . . . a month, maybe?"

Sundance nodded.

"Puts me to wondering," Hanks said with ponderous geniality, "if you're recovered yet. I figure you ain't. Could that be right?"

Sundance kept his eyes on Hanks's face. Lesson One, a long time ago, had been, don't bother watching the gun hand. You get your cue from the expression a split second before the hand goes into action.

"I guess we'll find out," Hanks went on. "Won't we?"

A wide-eyed boy on the other side of the street stood on tiptoe to peer past one of the small crowd of observers and took the situation in. "I'll get the new marshal," he said importantly to the man in front of him.

"Yeah, get him," the man said. The boy took a step away. The man grabbed him. "*After.*"

Hanks moved toward the center of the street; as Sundance had expected, he moved lithely. He circled around his opponent, then feinted his hand dartingly toward his gun butt. Sundance, still concentrating on Hanks's face, responded by tensing into a slight crouch, but did not attempt to draw. The sudden movement cost him another stab of pain. Hanks saw it reflected on his face and smiled.

"Hurts you, don't it?" he called. "Bet you're just a little *slow*, ain't you?" Sundance stared at him coldly, clenching his teeth against the pain.

They were now standing about twenty feet apart. Hanks suddenly turned and ran ten feet or so, stopped and turned again to face Sundance—just too far off for an accurate shot. Sundance moved toward him, each step now costing him pain and effort.

Hanks grinned broadly and sidled backward toward the edge of the street. Sundance started toward him, and again Hanks backed off. The maneuver was repeated, and repeated again.

Sundance's breath came heavily. He shook his head to clear his blurring vision; sweat was running into his eyes and stung them.

His quick movement to follow another crabwise dash by Hanks sent a needle of fire through his belly. He brushed his lower shirtfront with the fingers of his left hand, and could feel the dampness of seeping blood.

Along with the gallery of spectators, Butch had been moving down the plankwalk, keeping pace with the combatants; he saw the spreading stain on Sundance's shirt. He set a hand to his gun butt and called, "Come on, O.C.! Or *I'll* shoot you!"

Hanks stopped moving and looked at Sundance, taking in the beads of sweat on his forehead, the drawn expression, and the whitening face. Enough of the starch taken out of him, all right. He nodded. "I'm ready. Go for your gun."

Sundance shook his head, gasped once, and got out one word: "*You.*"

Hanks gave him a sardonic look and shook his head. Why, the shape this kid was in, he could practically let him clear leather before starting to make his move, and then take his own time about it.

Both men glanced involuntarily to the side of the street, where, from a store bearing the sign: JEWELER—CLOCKMAKER, several ornamental clocks on display suddenly emitted a medley of chimes.

Butch snapped a glance at the nearest clock face. The fancy kind, he thought, that play a little tune before they start striking the hour. . . . "It's five o'clock," he called to Hanks and Sundance. "Draw on the last chime."

They nodded, and settled into a half-crouch, now well within range of each other.

The first chime came, with hardly any difference in timing among the three or so clocks. That clockmaker pays good heed to his stock, Butch thought distractedly. Hanks's lips moved, as if he were counting.

Two.

Sundance seemed calmer now, almost relaxed.

Three.

Hanks's lips were still moving.

Four. Hanks frowned—was that four or . . . ? Hell with it! He pulled his pistol from its holster and slammed a shot toward Sundance.

A fraction of a second later, Sundance's hand, as if of its own accord, streaked for his gun, thumb automatically pulling back the hammer as it cleared the holster, letting go as the barrel came up to center on Hanks. The sound of the shot and the fifth chime of the clocks came together.

Sundance sagged as the echoes of the gunblast and the clock chimes died away.

Hanks, sprawled in the mud, was almost hidden by the swarm of onlookers crowding around him.

Butch came up to Sundance, who looked at him dazedly. "He drew early."

177

"I know," Butch said. "He never could count." It was not much of an epitaph, he realized, but better than many O.C. might have had from those who had known him best. At least it gave him the benefit of the doubt.

Sundance's mouth was half open, and the arm holding his pistol hung slackly at his side as he stared toward what he could see of Hanks through the crowd: mostly two skyward-pointing boot soles.

"He's dead," someone in the crowd muttered, an undertone of pleased excitement in his voice. "Got'm right in the *heart*."

Sundance winced and looked pleadingly at Butch. "I just wanted to put a hole in him. I didn't want to kill him. . . ."

"I know," Butch said.

"I hadda rush my *shot*."

Very gently, Butch took Sundance's shoulder and eased him around, then exerted just enough pressure to start him walking away from where Hanks lay. "I *know* . . ." he said again.

Sundance drew a long, hoarse breath, and another. He twitched out of Butch's grasp and ran for the side of the street, pounding across the plankwalk and into the alley beside the clockmaker's. Butch waited until the deep, retching sounds that came to him from the alley died away, then walked slowly to the edge of the store.

Sundance, on his knees, looked up at Butch. His eyes were watery, and he bore a shaken, sheepish look. "I never killed anybody before," he said wonderingly.

Butch looked at him in silent surprise.

"*Shot* 'em . . . never *killed* anybody. Arm, leg, hand, that's enough to put a man out of a fight, 's what I *meant* to . . . you *sure* he's dead?"

From where he stood at the corner of the building, Butch could now clearly see Hanks lying on his back.

The crowd had drawn back, evidently waiting for the law, the undertaker, or possibly the garbageman to do something about him. There was no suggestion in the way they stood that there was any question of a doctor's service's being required.

"We best get to our horses, Sundance," he said quietly. "We got some riding to do."

The boy who had wished to alert the law before the shootout and been detained by the considerate spectator—the circus never came to Circleville, so it would have been willful waste to put a stop to a real-life spectacle—burst into the marshal's office, yelling, "Marshal! Butch Cassidy and the Sundance Kid are in town. Sundance just shot a guy!"

He stopped, somewhat deflated. The office was empty, except for a pair of boots on the desk, and a white flat straw hat on the hatrack.

"I'll be right there," came a voice from the cells in the rear of the building.

The boy settled into a chair to wait. So far the new marshal, only in town a day or so, didn't seem to have any more get-up-and-go than old Ponder. Somebody like Bat Masterson, that'd be the kind of lawman to have around.

The marshal came in, and heard the boy's excited story impassively, while polishing one of the boots on the desk.

"Aren't you gonna go *after* 'em?" the boy asked.

"It's almost dark, and they'll be across the river by the time I can raise a posse," the marshal said indifferently. He set one boot down, satisfied with its gloss, and started on the other. "One thing about outlaws, son, they're dumb. You don't get 'em today, why, you'll get 'em tomorrow."

When the disappointed boy had left, the marshal, the second boot finished, placed it beside its mate, and looked abstractedly at them.

Butch Cassidy . . . the Sundance Kid. They were having a pretty good run of it now, but small-time stuff, not worth going to much trouble to bring them in for. Sooner or later, they'd cross that line, though, get puffed up and pull the job that made the difference.

When they did, Joe Le Fors would be ready for them.

The ford across the Sevier was tricky, but Butch knew it by heart. When they were on the east bank, they slowed, feeling safe from pursuit for the moment. In the dusk, the horses picked their way up a trail which grew gradually steeper.

"What was he like?" Sundance asked.

"Who?" Butch said, stifling a sigh. It was okay to have a conscience, a man wasn't much without one; but when something was done, it was done, and Sundance was letting this get to him too much.

"Hanks."

"Oh, Hanks." Butch looked for the words that would give a balanced assessment of the late O.C. "He was okay, really."

"*Thanks*," Sundance said heavily.

"What for?"

Sundance spoke with sudden violence. "I *wanted* you to tell me he was a lousy bastard who didn't deserve to live!"

"Oh."

A few painfully negotiated yards farther along the trail, Sundance asked, "He have any family?"

Jee-*sus*. "Just the five kids."

Sundance stopped his horse. "Did he?"

"No!" Butch said hotly. "Will you quit torturing yourself with this! He didn't *have* any kids. He didn't have a wife, just some hag he lived with. Far's I know, he didn't have any mother, not human, anyhow. He was a dirty, dumb, smelly rustler an' outlaw, and he

180

had his good parts an' his bad parts like everyone else, and he's dead, and that's an *end* to it. Sundance, you go around getting into gunfights, you just can't choose orphans to do it with!"

CHAPTER EIGHTEEN

"Along this way, gents. The cell we want's right at the end of the corridor."

Butch and Sundance walked ahead of the prison guard. Sundance felt undeniably oppressed and uneasy. If it weren't for these damn-fool city clothes he had on, he would have found it hard to shake off the impression that he and Butch were being shepherded to quarters assigned them for a term of years by a judge; it was the only thing that made wearing them worthwhile. Butch, on the other hand, seemed to glory in the situation, even the clothes, which he wore with a proud air. That dumb derby cocked over one ear . . . he'd practically fallen in love with it in the store, said it did something for him.

"You'll notice we got the latest *de*-vices," the guard said proudly. "Bars runnin' both down *and* crossways, made of case-hardened steel, as used in dreadnought armor platin'. Doors operated by electricity, for the smoothness of the workin', plus a single switch throwed in the warden's office locks 'em all tighter'n Sitting Bull's drum, in case of attempts at leavin' our happy home. No, sir, even if our guests had the wings of a angel, over these prison walls they ain't *about* to fly."

"Unless," Butch said cheerfully, "they got some topflight lawyers as can put right miscarriages of justice that has resulted in wrongful incarceration. Meaning no disrespect to the system, but the firm of Maxwell and Alonzo goes on the sacred principle that any man is innocent until proven guilty, especially one of our clients, in which case maybe not even then."

"Well, good luck to ya," the guard said. "What I hear, your man's up to the fetlocks in evidence. You cipher out some way to get him off at the trial you're sure will work, you might lemme know, so's I could get down a bet on it."

They were now at the cross-barred door of a cell, into which he inserted a key. Butch and Sundance, peering past him, could make out the figure of a man stretched on a cot. A deep, bubbling cough came from him, followed in a few seconds by a sour odor of old whiskey.

Butch looked quizzically at the guard, who carefully studied the far wall and after a moment said, "A man that has a complaint of the lungs is entitled to a little medication, an' if the doctors won't prescribe . . ."

"*And* if he's got a little spare change, eh?" Butch's tone was heartily man-to-man. "Good to know our client's so well looked after."

"Someone to see you, Cassidy," the guard called.

The figure on the cot stirred and hitched itself around until a pallid hollow-eyed face was turned toward the cell door. "I don't know nobody . . ." it mumbled, the eyes unfocused.

"It's your lawyers."

"Lawyers . . . ?"

The guard reached for a metal plate on the wall and pushed a knife switch up. The barred door slid open, and he gestured to Butch and Sundance to enter the cell.

"When you want outta here," he said, "just holler."

Butch bowed slightly toward him, the very picture of an attorney acknowledging a courtesy. "Thank you."

The guard threw the switch and the door slid shut with an emphatic clang. Sundance took a deep breath.

The jail he'd been in at Sundance had been homey and cheerful, compared to this. Suppose these folks, with all their electricity and stuff, were to find out any minute that Attorney Alonzo and Attorney Maxwell were Butch Cassidy and the Sundance Kid? Those doors would *never* open again.

The cell's inmate sat on the edge of his cot and blinked blearily up at them. "There must be a mistake . . . I don't have no . . ."

Butch's face settled into lines of profound sadness as he looked at Mike Cassidy—at what had been Mike Cassidy. The once-alert face was seamed and stubbly; the eyes were bloodshot and seemed not to take anything in clearly; and . . . the right sleeve of his shirt was empty and clumsily pinned up.

"It's me, Mike," he said softly. "Butch."

It hurt him a good deal that it took Mike a full three second to reply, and hazily at that. "Butch . . . ?"

"Cassidy," Butch said.

The ravaged face slowly took on an expression of delight as recognition spread across it. "Butch? Butch Cassidy!"

Butch glanced around quickly. It wasn't likely that anyone could hear, but this was definitely the wrong place for his name to be dropped. "Not so *loud* . . ."

Mike Cassidy pushed himself off the cot with his left arm and tottered to his feet, stumbled toward Butch, grabbed his right hand with his own left, then hugged him. Butch stood his ground, inwardly recoiling from the combined aroma of booze and long-unwashed Mike that enveloped him.

"Look at ya, Butch . . . just look at ya . . ." Butch glanced at Sundance, who *was* looking at him, and with some distaste at that. Butch could read his expression all too plainly: *This* is *your* hero?

"'Member them days back on your pa's ranch, Butch? Taught ya what I knew, ever' damn thing," Mike said happily, still clutching. "How t' cut critters out of a herd, the runnin' an, how t' deal with them slick buyers over to Green River? The good days, huh, you an' me, Butch? Butch, you c'n see that it ain't gone so well with me lately, I been a bit down on the luck—out on a limb, too, some feller told me, 's a pretty good joke, you get it, about not having no arm anymore? . . . But, say, I guess you're out of that kind of game, ain't you, Butch? Ya *made* somethin' of yourself, boy—you're a lawyer!"

"No, no, I'm not," Butch said rapidly. "I'm not a lawyer."

Mike's seamed face looked at him blankly. "You're not? Then what're ya doin'—"

Butch bent closer to him and in a near-whisper said, "We're gonna get you out of here."

Sundance looked at the cross-barred door with its electrically operated lock, and the dress-stone walls, floor, and ceiling, and said with an air of mild interest, "Out of *here*?"

Mike stepped back from Butch and looked at his visitors. He took in and let out a deep breath and shook his head to clear it. For the first time during the visit, Butch could see the remnants of the firmness and dash that had made this man . . . God! He couldn't be more than forty-seven or so, for all he looked a battered sixty—his boyhood idol. "Listen, I appreciate this," Mike said in a low voice. "But you can't bust me out. I ain't up to it." He waved his left hand toward the pinned-up right sleeve.

"There's *other* ways to get you out, Mike," Butch said. "We're gonna get you a lawyer—a *real* lawyer— the best lawyer," he went on, warming to the idea and speaking in an expansive tone that gave Sundance a premonitory shiver, "in the state of Wyoming!"

Mike blinked at him; Sundance scanned the floor as though searching for a spittoon.

"*Cyrus Antoon*, if we have to!"

Sundance's head snapped up. "Come on! *Antoon?* You know what he *gets?*"

"Yeah," Butch said. "What he gets is, he gets his clients off."

"But his goddam *fees!* You got any notion of *them?*"

"No. How much?"

"I don't know. But a lot."

Butch gave a tight grin and ran a hand up the back of his neck, tilting the derby forward to a more rakish angle. "We'll take it out of the bank," he said gently.

Sundance briefly wondered if his wound were troubling him, but decided that hanging with Butch was enough to make your stomach hurt even if you weren't gut-shot. "*What* bank?"

Mike peered in confusion from one of his visitors to the other. Butch had been a nice boy, quick learner, but he seemed to have gotten pretty confused as he grew up.

"Whichever one we pick," Butch said.

Once you have said that Montpelier, Idaho, is in Bear Lake County, is a touch nearer the county seat, Paris, than it is to Bear Lake or to the towns of Dingle and Raymond, and that any Montpelierite in reasonable shape can take a stroll out from town to the Bear River, you have said more than ninety-nine out of a hundred people know, or would want to know, about it. For Butch and Sundance it had another element of interest: the First National Bank of Montpelier.

The First National Bank was located on Main Street. And Main Street, Montpelier, as Butch had discovered by looking at a poster in the railroad station to which he and Sundance had repaired for a conference after the Alonzo & Maxwell consultation with Mike Cassidy, was where the Famous Colonel Blanyard Carnival and Dog and Pony Show Together With Educational Wonders of the Ages would be doing business in three days.

"In case the robbery don't come off, we can go an' console ourselves with an afternoon of harmless amusement, is that it?" Sundance asked. He eyed another poster. "Why don't we go to Salt Lake, then? Buffalo Bill'll be there, and we could see some tame desperadoes an' Indians doin' their stuff, maybe pick up a few tips."

"We don't wanta watch the show," Butch said. "But you can bet your ass that a lotta folks will, and that's our edge."

Sundance sighed. "With you, I *always* get the feeling I'm betting my ass. And I can't help suspicioning the wheel is rigged."

Sundance had to admit that Colonel Blanyard was doing a great job of distracting the attention of the townsfolk of Montpelier. They were turned out in larger numbers than he would have suspected the town held: gawping at the trained dogs and ponies, the discouraged elephant, and the Educational Wonders (especially the Wonder in an enclosed tent, admission a quarter, gentlemen only, who undertook to demonstrate the exotic dances of the Ouled Naïl); pouring rivers of nickles and dimes into the outstretched palms of the proprietors of games of chance and skill; consuming phosphates, cotton candy, snow cones, candy apples, and unhealthy-looking bright red sausages held between halves of a long roll; imperiling the digestion of these treats by being spun rapidly in the air in gaudily colored steam-powered machines; and gasping and screaming at the efforts of a spunky-looking lady traversing Main Street on a wire stretched twenty feet above it.

The one thing none of these people seemed to be doing was paying any attention to him and Butch as they carried a large metal money box through the crowd toward the bank; and for this he was profoundly grateful.

In the anteroom of the bank, the two armed guards looked up as Butch and Sundance entered with their burden. One leaned negligently against a wall; the other sat at a counter behind which was a board with a number of hooks, from several of which revolvers and shotguns hung.

"*Hi,*" Butch said brightly. "Got a big deposit to make here."

"Fine," the guard against the wall said. "They like that, gettin' deposits. What they're in business for. Just hand over your guns first."

Butch licked his lips. "We're s'posed to guard this money till it's safe in the vault, that's what our boss said."

"An' we're s' posed to take your guns, that's what *our* boss said." The guard's gently reasonable tone was reinforced by a hand sliding to his gun butt.

Sundance looked uneasily at Butch. Butch thought for an instant, then reached for his pistol. Sundance tensed . . . but Butch reversed his weapon and handed it butt first to the guard, who passed it on to his colleague behind the counter, who in turn hung it from a vacant peg behind him. Butch jerked his head toward Sundance, who reluctantly gave up his own gun.

The standing guard, after giving the pistol to his colleague, stepped to a window facing the street as another roar came from the crowd watching the wire walker.

"Two bits says she don't make it."

"How far's she got?" the guard behind the counter asked.

The first guard craned his neck. "Can't see too good from here."

A noise midway between a shriek and a shout came to them.

"*Damn,* I'd like to see that," the second guard said. He opened the door into the main area of the bank;

Butch and Sundance carried the box inside. They glanced back, and saw that the first guard was now leaning out the front door. Another braying yell of delight or horror or both came from the crowd.

"I *gotta* see this," they heard the guard say. "Be right back."

Butch flashed a meaning glance at Sundance as they entered the main area of the bank. Sundance ignored it, and, after a look around which revealed the presence of a scattering of customers, two tellers, and the manager, muttered under his breath, "No guns. *Good*, Butch. What're we supposed to do—strangle everybody?"

Butch squinted at a dour-looking woman and a boy of about eight coming toward them. "We set the box down, now," he muttered.

Sundance bent with Butch until the strongbox rested on the floor, then straightened. "That mean we're giving up on this?" he asked hopefully.

Butch ignored him, and elaborately pretended to ignore the boy, who was industriously chomping caramel-covered popcorn from a paper bag—evidently he and his mother had tarried at the carnival before coming to the bank. As the boy passed behind him, Butch contrived to skid on the polished marble floor and ram him hard enough to knock the bag of popcorn out of his hand.

In an instant, Butch was on his knees, scooping up the scattered confection and showering apologies. "I'm *sorry*, I didn't see . . ." He reached into his pocket. "Here—here's a nickle, buy yourself another bag." He gave the staring kid a wide smile as he pressed the coin on him.

The boy's mother peered down at him over the yard of whalebone that stiffened her front, and said flatly, "It's a dime."

Butch recalled clearly a sign out in the street that had read CARAMEL POPCORN 5¢, but realized that there are times when you have to spend money to make money. He dug into his pocket again and said expansively, "Here's twenty cents. Buy *two* bags. I'm sorry, ma'am . . ."

The boy's fist closed around the coins and he gave Butch a gap-toothed grin. The mother contented herself with a cold nod as she stepped past him, her son in tow, and went through the door to the anteroom.

Sundance, who had watched this byplay with bewilderment, felt a positive chill as Butch, with a smile that struck him as suited to a maniac, now shook the bag and scattered what reamined of the popcorn onto the floor. In school back in New Jersey, they had made him read a lot of stuff that was hard to take in and that he thought he had managed to forget, but one line from some play about a fellow with family problems came back to him unbidden: "O, what a noble mind is here o'erthrown." Not to say that Butch's mind was even at its best so noble, but it certainly seemed to have been thrown and hog-tied.

Gone lunatic or not, Butch was still in charge; and Sundance obeyed the gesture of his leader's head that seemed meant to direct him to move to the wall alongside the door. His eyes widened with comprehension—and relief—as Butch blew into the paper bag, twisted its neck shut, and slammed his palm hard against it.

Sundance estimated the noise the bursting bag made as about the equivalent of a .22 being fired, nothing heavier; but it was enough to bring the one remaining guard boiling out of the anteroom, gun held at the ready just where Sundance could pluck it away as he passed; a kick to the knee sent the guard sprawling; and Sundance, glorying in the familiar heft of the weapon in his hand, whirled and moved it gently back and forth, covering the bank's customers and tellers.

"All *right*, folks," he said. "This'll just take a few minutes. Just put your hands against the walls and don't move."

With a sudden surge of delight, he saw that the huge vault at the rear of the room was open, the manager standing frozen with astonishment in front of it. "*You* can move," he called. "Away from that door, *fast*, an' don't lay a *hand* on it unless you want a extra belly button."

The manager scuttled away ten paces, then returned to face the wall and place his hands against it, following the example of his employees and patrons.

Butch strode jauntily toward the vault; Sundance followed him, back up, eyes and pistol barrel moving back and forth, alert for any unwise moves.

Butch pulled the door fully open. Sundance glanced over his shoulder and beheld a treasure trove. Fat piles of bills in neat wrappings and plump canvas coin bags crowded each other from the floor almost to the ceiling. Sundance regarded the spectacle with joy and regret, the regret coming from his realization that it would take a strong cart, and probably Colonel Blanyard's elephant hauling it, to clear the whole thing out. But there was enough portable booty there to make two hard-working outlaws happy and prosperous well into the next administration.

"You keep covering everybody," Butch said.

Sundance nodded, his eyes gleaming. Butch went to the vault, pulled down several stacks of bills, gave them a fast riffle to verify the amounts written on ther paper wrappers, and stepped back.

"What're you doing?" Sundance said, looking past him to the scarcely diminished hoard.

"I got enough," Butch said.

"*Enough?*" Sundance cried. "There ain't no such *thing* as enough, you're talkin' about money. What d'you *mean*, enough?"

"To cover Antoon's fee."

"Are you crazy?" Sundance said hotly; "when are we gonna get a chance like *this* again?"

"It's all we need," Butch said firmly. "I told you, I'm trying to go straight."

Sundance looked wildly around the bank, at the customers and employees patiently leaning against the walls, supported by their palms, at the scatter of popcorn and the burst paper on the marble floor, at the open door of the vault, and briefly at the stolen pistol he held. He gritted his teeth to keep back a low whine of rage and frustration. "You call *this* going straight?" he said in low, venomous tones. "Stealing a *little*?"

"It's close enough," Butch said.

Sundance had considered the question still open for debate; but to his horror, Butch pushed against the vault door, which ponderously began to swing closed. Sundance lunged for it, even felt the edge scrape the tips of his fingers . . . but it slammed shut, and there was a very final-sounding click from inside.

"You got the *key* to this?" he called furiously to the manager.

"Time lock," the official said nervously. "Close it that way, which you're not supposed to, won't open for twenty-four hours. A precaution the . . ." Catching Sundance's mordant eye, he elected not to continue his explanation of the measures the vault manufacturer had taken to thwart thieves.

Sundance glared at the closed vault door, then walked to where Butch was dropping the stacks of bills he had taken into the tin money box. Sundance said nothing as the task was completed—all too quickly, in his view, considering what might have been; the damn box wasn't a third full—and reacted only by closing his eyes briefly when Butch padlocked the box shut.

As Butch bent to pick up the box, Sundance said savagely, "Ain't you forgetting something?"

Butch looked up. "What?"

Sundance jerked his head toward the customers, tellers, manager, and guard, still standing with their hands to the wall.

"Oh. Right."

"Going straight—*part* straight—is one thing, but I hope you ain't going so far as to *try* to get caught."

Butch ignored the jibe and spoke up sharply. "You people! Into the manager's office! And stay there ten minutes, not a peep out of you! We're leavin' a man on guard who'll fill the room full of lead if he hears a sound!"

When the captives were herded in, Butch turned a key in the door. "They'll start gettin' brave in about five minutes," he observed, "but that'll be enough time. Come on."

He took the strongbox and made for the anteroom, a glowering Sundance following. As they came into it, the first guard entered from the street.

"She make it across—that wire walker?" Butch asked cheerfully.

The guard appeared disappointed as he answered, "Yeah." He looked behind the counter. "Where's Barney?"

"Who?"

"The other guard."

"Oh. He's inside."

Sundance moved past Butch to open the outer door, and stood aside to let him pass through. As Butch crossed the threshold, the guard called, "Hey, you! Hold on a minute!"

They stopped and turned slowly. Sundance's hand opened, ready to dart inside his coat for the pistol he had taken from the guard inside, now tucked awkwardly into his trousers top. Butch calculated the chances of heaving the money box at the guard before he could get a shot off . . . not good.

"You forgot your guns," the guard said, holding them out butt first with a reproving smile.

CHAPTER NINETEEN

Hat brims tilted over their faces against the late-afternoon sun, Butch and Sundance sat on the railroad-station bench watching the Southern Pacific paymaster and an attendant guard set up a table and chair next to the tracks.

Butch's eyes brightened when the two men lifted a heavy box onto the table and the guard unlocked and lifted the lid; even from where they sat, the piles of bills and stacks of coins were visible.

"You figure out how we're gonna take that?" Sundance asked.

"Not yet. Today we'll just see how they do everything, so's I can work it out. Same routine every day, likely. Right about this part of it looks promising, they'd hardly be expecting any trouble. That guard looks downright sleepy."

"Ain't much going on, for sure." Sundance glanced around the station platform. A few bums, some Chinese women waiting for their men on the S.P. work crew, and a couple of cowboys loitered there. One of the punchers was working the shell-and-pea game, but evidently to pass the time more than to make money; a pair of the Chinese women were shrilly amused at their inability to pick the shell under which the pea was hidden.

"Jury should of come in by now on Mike," Sundance observed. "Hope it went okay for him."

"With Antoon, it will have," Butch said. The Nevada papers had not given much space to the Mike Cassidy trial in Wyoming, but Butch and Sundance had been able to follow its general progress. Evidently Cyrus Antoon had earned his considerable fee, cross-examining witnesses until they denied their own testimony, and producing witnesses of his own who placed Mike long distances away from the scenes of his various alleged crimes. He had also been completely successful in having ruled as inadmissible any comments linking the Montpelier bank robbery with the arrangements for Mike's defense, which was even more of an achievement.

The work train, pulled by a small engine, came in sight down the track, two open cars crammed with laborers. Butch glanced at the station clock: just past six. Something like a five-minute stretch, when it came time to do the job, to get the money and be away before the work crew arrived. The workmen would have to go without their wages for a day when they pulled it off, but the S.P. would make it up pretty quick—railroad workers had long since made it clearly understood that no pay or slow pay meant mysterious disruptions of train service.

The work train pulled into the station, and the men, about half of them Chinese—no, not all men, Butch and Sundance saw; a good many were obviously no more than ten or twelve—began jumping off and making for the pay table.

"Look at that," Butch said. "Little kids . . ."

Sundance nodded and rose. Butch followed him as they went to mingle with the throng of dirty, wary laborers. Butch noted that the men were paid with bills, the boys with coins.

Butch was aware of a man falling into step beside him, flanked by another. "Hey, Butch."

Butch halted the instinctive reach for his pistol as he turned and saw who had addressed him. "Harvey. What're you doin'?"

Harvey Logan nodded toward the man next to him. "Me an' Carver been workin' this train crew. Y'know, to see what we could pick up?"

"And?"

"Word has it," Logan said impressively, "There's a train fulla money leaving Frisco next week."

Sundance had been edgily silent since the appearance of the two men, but now spoke up. "Who's this?"

Butch turned to him. "This is old Harvey Logan, sometimes known as Kid Curry, and Bill Carver." To the others he said, "Bill, Harvey . . . the Sundance Kid."

"Pleasure," Logan said.

Carver nodded at Sundance, then said to Butch, "We ain't told you the best part. It's the damn mint train!"

"What's that?" Sundance asked.

"There's a mint in Frisco, right?" Logan said patiently. "Well, ever' so often they take a whole bunch of brand-new money they just printed up, an' they ship it out. . . ."

"And this train . . . ?" Sundance said eagerly.

". . . leaves next Thursday for Salt Lake."

Butch turned the idea over in his mind for a moment, shook his head, and reluctantly said, "I'll pass."

"Okay, *pass*," Sundance said. "We don't need you, anyway." He leaned past Butch and said to Carver and Logan, "I'll do it with you guys."

Butch gave him a pitying look. "Which one of you is going to *plan* this robbery?"

"*I* am!" Sundance said angrily. "You think you're the only one who can lead?"

Butch gave each of his three companions a measured glance. "Around here, yes."

Sundance looked at him with irritation. "In other words, we can't even rob a train without you showing us how, is that it?"

"That's right," Butch said complacently.

"Then *show* us how!" Sundance almost yelled. Carver and Logan looked on with interest. This new friend of Cassidy's seemed to be the real Tabasco when it came to temper.

Butch surveyed him for a moment, and nodded. "All right."

The foreman of the jury cleared his throat, unfolded the slip of paper that he held in his hand, and read from it. The message was simple, but he felt that it was due the dignity of his position to consult the actual document rather than delivering it, so to speak, offhand.

"We the jury find the defendant, Mike Cassidy . . . not guilty."

There were murmurs, but no cheers—or boos—from the spectators in the courtroom.

Cyrus Antoon allowed a pleased smile to crease his bland, well-barbered face as he turned to his client. Mike Cassidy, looking somewhat nearer to his former self after a month's drying-out on Antoon's orders, and neatly attired, grinned at his attorney.

"This is a great country, Mr. Antoon! Here I am, guilty as hell and a free man!"

Antoon's smile turned wintry—like the fictitious firm of Alonzo & Maxwell, he considered his clients by definition innocent, with his main function being to find, or construct, the facts that would prove them so—but he grasped Mike's left hand with his right, pumped it briefly, and left. The likes of Cyrus Antoon and Mike Cassidy, he reflected, could have only a professional relationship, never a social one. It occurred to him that he would rather not meet Cassidy when the latter was plying his trade.

Had he had two hands, Mike would have rubbed them gleefully as he started to leave the courtroom. He glanced up at the press gallery, and was pleased to see Ray Bledsoe there, beckoning to him. A man needed someone to unwind with after what he'd been through, and old Ray was the right sort—lawman, but with a reasonable understanding of the fellows on the other side. After all, if it wasn't for Mike, and others like him, what would the Bledsoes do for a living?

Bledsoe waited for him at the top of the spiral staircase leading to the gallery. Mike looked past him and saw a painter setting to work, now that the crowd was departing, on a mural that incorporated Custer's Last Stand and a combine harvester, probably meant to represent the Old and the New.

"How in the hell *are* ya, Ray?" Mike greeted him. "What d'ya say we go on down to some saloon here an' get ourselves drunk?"

"You're not gettin' drunk, Mike," the sheriff said levelly. "Not until you do this, anyway."

"Do what?" Mike said, having so far thought that he'd done all that could be expected of him, sitting quietly while Antoon worked his forensic magic.

"I got a pretty good idea Butch Cassidy robbed the Montpelier Bank to pay for Antoon," Bledsoe said, narrowly watching Mike for any sign of guilty knowledge.

"Oh, God *bless* him," Mike said, his eyes filling with ready tears.

Bledsoe, a little taken aback by the artless response, continued doggedly. "So I figure you owe him something."

"I do, Ray . . . everything. Lemme know—"

Bledsoe took from his coat a document written on stiff paper and embossed toward the bottom with a number of official-looking seals. "I got the governors of three states to agree that if Butch'll come in voluntarily—*right now*—they'll drop all past charges against him."

"That's great . . ." Mike said vaguely. "Them governors are generous men, what you call large-hearted."

"It'd be great if I knew where the hell he is!" Bledsoe said. He looked at Mike. "*You* can find him. People'll tell you things they won't tell me." But can you remember them? he asked himself. He shook off the discouraging thought and handed Mike the document. "You get this to him—and do it fast—because if he does *one* more thing, it's all off."

Mike regarded the paper with an air of alert, informed interest. What it said he had no way of knowing, but he had long since learned by observation how people who actually could read looked at such things.

"Well, get going!" Bledsoe said impatiently. As Mike scurried down the staircase, reaching across his body with his left arm to grasp the outer rail, the sheriff looked worriedly after him. If Mike's wits hadn't been softened for good by booze, and if he didn't pitch over his horse's head and break his neck, maybe he'd catch up with Butch before it was too late. . . .

In another part of the gallery Joe Le Fors pushed his straw skimmer to the back of his head and looked at Mike's retreating back. He said quietly, "I don't have to go along with this amnesty thing Bledsoe's cooked up." He nodded his head toward Mike, now on the main floor and heading for an exit door. "When he leads us to Cassidy—we grab him."

Mike urged his spavined horse to a stop, which was a good deal easier than it had been to keep it going along the track from Circleville. From the directions he'd been given, this was the place . . . but it did not bear the signs of life that a woman and two active boys should have set on it. He slid from his horse, clumped up on the porch, and knocked on the front door. "Hello?"

There was silence, and he pounded on the door with his fist. Again, no answer. He tried the door latch, and, when it lifted and the door slid back on its hinges a crack, he stepped inside the cabin.

The front room held no furniture, no sign that a

family had ever been there. At first glance the bedroom presented the same impression; then Mike stepped back and drew a sharp breath as he saw an untidy bundle wrapped in a patchwork quilt lying on the floor.

Mike stepped quietly over to the sleeping figure and bent down, then jumped away as a flurry of motion resolved itself into a wide-awake and glaring old man sitting up and holding a gun pointed at him.

"Get outta my *house*!" this apparition said.

"This ain't your house . . . it's the Parkers'," Mike replied, earnestly hoping that the directions he had been given were correct.

"Mine now," the old man said. "They left. I helped 'em pack the wagon. Now get outta here!"

Mike backed away. "They left? Who?"

"The woman and the kids."

"Wasn't a man around? The husband . . . ?"

"Nope." The old man shook his head. "She said he was dead."

CHAPTER TWENTY

The high sun glinted blindingly off the S.P. tracks as they curved through a rock gorge, straightened out, and arrowed past where Butch and Sundance stood on a promontory surveying them.

"I been thinkin'," Sundance said.

"That could be dangerous." Butch continued to study the rail line.

"I been thinkin'," Sundance repeated, as if there had been no comment worth taking notice of, "what do we need Logan an' Carver for? Why don't we take this train alone?"

"Because you can't rob a train with two men, that's why," Butch said patiently. "It takes four, minimum. Anyway, stupid, by now they've *boarded* the train in Winnemucca."

Sundance peered past him. "Looks like they missed it."

Butch spun and saw Carver and Logan riding hard toward them, their horses heavily lathered and evidently close to foundering.

He and Sundance ran toward the two riders, who now slowed and stopped, almost toppling from their mounts as Butch and Sundance reached for the reins.

"The goddam thing never *stopped*," Logan panted. He sank to the ground, his chest heaving. "Just high-balled right on through."

"Without nobody on board," Carver panted, "we can't make the engineer stop it."

"We could pull up some track," Sundance suggested, "derail it."

Butch shook his head. "No. That's messy . . . people could get killed." Logan and Carver exchanged looks, silently agreeing that there were problems in working with a man who thought you could make an omelette without breaking eggs.

Logan had finally caught his breath and was able to speak normally. "You ain't heard the *best* part." He paused to give the news weight. "There's a detachment of cavalry on the train."

"Cavalry?" Sundance said.

Logan nodded. "Cavalry. Whole carload full . . . horses in a cattle car ahead. I guess to pertect the shipment."

Sundance jammed his hands in his trouser pockets and glared at the ground. "Well, that blows it." Logan and Carver grumbled agreement.

"Not necessarily," Butch said.

They turned and looked at Butch. He gave them a cheerful smile from where he sat on a rock, tossing pebbles into the gorge below.

"I hearn he's thinkin' of—"

"They was word that—"

"Kid Curry an' Bill Carver was s'posed ta—"

"Ain't nothin' *definite*, but it seems—"

Mike rode away from the saloon in Brown's Hole, digesting the information the friendly young outlaws had given him. Nothing certain about any of it, but it was pointing in one direction, a direction it would be a good idea to head in. He held his horse tightly with his knees as his one hand fumbled inside his jacket to reassure him that the tri-state amnesty offer was still there. It was Butch's chance for a steady life, and, as Ray Bledsoe had said, Mike owed him that.

Preoccupied, he did not see the three riders who followed him at a distance, though a fitful gleam of sunlight picked out the white straw hat their leader wore.

The tracks stretched out in a straight line behind and ahead of them, the one clear feature in the expanse of flat desert, still indistinct in the predawn light.

Butch stood between the rails, deep in thought. Logan, Carver, and Sundance huddled by the horses, watching him, wondering what Cassidy the Planner has hatching.

"Butch," Logan said, "that train's gonna be along in a couple hours."

"I know."

"Then what in the hell are we doing way out here?" Sundance demanded.

Butch looked over at him. "A place like this is where they'd least expect us to hit them."

"This is where *I'd* least expect us to hit 'em!" Sundance said hotly. "Are you crazy? You can't rob a train out here. No more'n you would on a bridge."

"Well, not *right* here," Butch said.

Logan took a step forward. "They'll *see* us! They're not gonna stop for a bunch of guys sitting on horses by the tracks. We'd *look* like train robbers, and I don't s'pose they'd wanna stop an' see if they was misjudgin' us."

"You're right," Butch observed. "We gotta get rid of the horses."

Sundance snorted. "Get rid of the horses? What're we gonna do after we rob the train, run? There's cavalry on board!"

Butch looked at them, his jaw set. "This is going to work. And after we've done it you're all going to be famous. Because people are going to talk about this train robbery for a long, long time."

Logan and Carver regarded him with eager, if dubious, interest; Sundance looked away.

"I got one question," Logan said. "After we get rid of the horses—which, by the way, sounds crazier'n hell to me—*how* we gonna stop this train?"

Butch, following the tradition of born teachers going back as far as Socrates, answered the question with another: "What does a train have to stop for?"

Carver spoke up for the first time. "Passengers?"

Butch, Logan, and even Sundance looked sharply at him, all sharing the thought that if this train *had* stopped to pick up passengers, he and Logan would have been on it at Winnemucca, and this whole session would not have been necessary.

Logan shook his head disgustedly. "You dumb . . ." He snapped his fingers and addressed Butch. *"Coal."*

"No."

"Well, they ain't usin' wood no more, so it can't be that. . . ." Carver lapsed into silence, trying to work out the puzzle.

"All right, smartass," Sundance said. "Then what?"

Butch looked at them with a gentle smile. "Water."

Mike Cassidy hurried back to his horse, which he had left tethered a little away from where the S.P. crew was re-laying a section of track. The heathen Chinee, as the poet called them, had been friendly enough, but hadn't had all that much information to give. The scraps he had gathered, though, fit in with what he'd heard at Brown's Hole. It wouldn't be long before he could get to Butch—and, from the sound of things, only just in time.

He reached out his left hand for his horse's reins, then took in the fact that a man wearing a flat white straw hat was standing patiently by the animal's head.

"Where is he?" Le Fors said.

Mike, not really hoping it would do any good, feigned innocence. "Beg pardon?"

"Butch. Where is he?"

204

"I don't know." Well, it was only half a lie. "And if I knew," he went on defiantly, "I still wouldn't tell ya. Even if you killed me."

The sudden appearance of the gun in Le Fors's hand chilled him. This machinelike manhunter was after Butch, the boy he'd taught the tricks of the trade, the man who had come to his rescue and miraculously kept him from a prison term that would have amounted to a death sentence . . . and Mike Cassidy had the chance to throw off the downhill years of boozing and weakness, and make a stand to help Butch. . . .

The hammer on Le Fors's gun clicked back.

"The mint train!" Mike said.

The old man checked his watch. Only seven minutes now until the train was due. His eyes went to the water tank by the tracks, the tallest structure—the only one, not counting the shanty he shared with his wife—for miles around. Everything in order, the spout at the bottom of the tank ready to refill the locomotive's boiler. His gaze drifted past the tank to the tiny garden in front of his house, where his wife was bending to chop some weeds with a hoe. Later, he'd dump out a little of the water left in the tank; the garden was looking pretty dry. Against S.P. rules, but the company would never know. Likely they expected it, anyway.

Inside the tank, Logan, Carver, and Sundance looked at Butch disgustedly, irritated as much by his cheerful air as by the fact that they had been standing in water up to their chests for an hour and a half. A frying pan holding a water-tight canister bobbed on the water in front of them.

Butch cocked his head, straining to listen.

"This is the last train I'm ever robbing with you, Butch," Sundance said.

Butch held up one hand. "I hear it."

"About time," Sundance said. "We been in here so long my legs is numb."

Logan spoke up. "I gotta take a leak real bad."

Carver gave a quick look around, and lowered his eyes. "I just did."

The others looked with distaste at the water they were standing in, then stiffened as the sound of a distant train whistle came to them. Logan and Carver glanced quickly at each other.

Butch caught the exchange of looks. "You're not having second thoughts?"

Logan squinted at him, then shook his head. "I'm the one who told you about it in the first place, ain't I?"

"I just want to make sure."

They could hear the sound of the locomotive plainly now, and the surface of the water rippled as the vibration of the train's approach was transmitted through the ground to the tank's supporting legs. The chugging slowed as it approached the tank, and a piercing shriek of brakes sounded from almost beneath them.

They could follow what was happening from the noises outside: the clank of the locomotive's water dome being opened, a murmur of conversation between the tank man and the engineer, a more distant hubbub of voices that would be the soldiers and passengers getting off for a brief stretch, the rattle of the spout's chain as it was guided to the water dome.

The level of water in the tank began to drop. Sundance reached for the floating frying pan, quickly stripped tape from the canister, took out two heavy bandoliers of ammunition and looped them over his shoulders.

Voices sounded almost from underneath them. "Sounds like a lot of 'em," Logan muttered.

"Enough," Butch said.

Panic flared in Logan's face as he whispered, "We can't take that many on!"

Butch bared his teeth and whispered, "We won't *have* to if you all do your jobs right!"

Logan cast a worried glance at Carver, who looked as unhappy as he did. The water was now down to knee level; it stopped there. They heard a clank—that would be the engine's water dome closing and being dogged shut—and the spout chain rattling as it was returned to its place.

An ear-splitting whistle came from the engine, and the sound of voices began to die away as the passengers and soldiers obeyed its summons and reboarded the train.

A hiss of steam and a powerful coughing belch from the engine announced the first slow turn of the mighty driving wheels. Butch reached up and grasped the top of the tank. "Okay? Here we go!"

He pulled himself up and balanced on the rim of the tank, then jumped onto the top of the barely moving express car behind the tender, teetered slightly, and quickly knelt, holding on hard. A thump behind him told him that Sundance had followed and was in place.

But . . . He looked back at the slowly receding tank. The disembodied heads of Logan and Carver appeared above its rim. "*Jump,* you lousy . . ." Butch muttered.

Logan and Carver sent him apologetic waves, and sank out of sight.

The train was gathering speed now, and the water tank dwindled in the distance as Butch and Sundance regarded it disgustedly.

"You're getting to be the only person I can depend on anymore," Butch said.

"I coulda told you that. Think two of us can do it?"

"I don't know." Butch ran his eye down the three cars behind him and the engine and tender ahead. "I guess we'll find out."

He and Sundance looked at each other for a moment, weighing the chances. "Okay," Butch said, "I'll take the engineer and fireman and you go pull the pin between the cattle car and the cavalry."

Sundance nodded and moved back along the top of the express car, his body low, grabbing onto the narrow walkway to steady himself.

Butch picked his way along the car toward the tender and engine. God *damn* Harve and Carver, he thought. They expect a cut for helping set this up, they can go pee up a rope! There's any justice, they'll drown in that tank. . . .

Hanging by his fingers, Logan twisted his head to look down, gauging the distance to the ground. A drop, but not too much. He let go and yelled as he fell onto the waterspout, straddling it painfully. It yielded slowly and dumped him to the ground, soaking him with a gush of water.

Carver landed on the suddenly muddy ground beside him. They picked themselves up and began trudging toward the distant gorge where their horses were hidden.

The old water-tank tender looked after them with mild interest. They didn't look like the class of man that's so desperate for a bath they'd take one in a water tank, but you never could tell.

Butch scrabbled his way along the coal-heaped tender, morosely aware that his soaked clothes were gathering and holding a remarkable quantity of coal dust. He peered into the engine cab. Good: the fireman was calmly stoking the firebox, the engineer was relaxed at the throttle, peering ahead down the line; no suspicion yet.

He jumped down into the cab with gun drawn and called to the engineer, "Just keep it going."

The engineer looked around, puffed on his pipe calmly, and nodded. "That's what I thought I'd do." He smiled amiably at Butch. "You picked the wrong train to rob, friend. We got a whole contingent of U.S. Cavalry aboard."

Butch returned the smile even more amiably. "Not for long, we don't."

The engineer and fireman exchanged questioning looks.

Amid a rattle of displaced coal, Sundance jumped down into the cab, as dirty and disheveled as Butch, and panting heavily. "Problems . . ." he gasped.

"What?"

"Harve said the car with the horses was in *front* of the car with the soldiers?"

"Butch nodded.

"The other way around. It's behind."

The engineer chuckled and sucked on his pipe.

Butch frowned. "We'll have to change our plans a bit."

"I imagine so," the engineer said.

"Slow the train down. Be ready to stop when I tell you."

The engineer smiled broadly. "You boys want to get off? I don't believe there'll be any trouble about collectin' your fares." He flinched and his smile was wiped away as he felt the steely chill of the barrel of Sundance's pistol being shoved against his head.

Sundance murmured, low but dangerous, "He said *slow* the train."

The engineer hurriedly reached for his controls.

Butch asked, "Think you can keep the cavalry in their car for a while, Sundance?"

Sundance nodded.

"You're gonna have to make it seem like there's more than one of you."

"Sure. How many do you want me to be?" Sundance reached for the reserve pistol at Butch's waist, checked the cylinder, and shook his head. "Lucky you didn't have to fire this—your bullets are all wet." He shook the ruined loads out and began replacing them with fresh cartridges from one of the bandoliers on his shoulders. "Give me about two minutes to get back there and get ready."

He jumped up onto the tender and began working his way rearward. He hopped across the gap between the express car and the first coach, thankful that the train had now begun to slow, and moved to the rear of the coach. Kneeling on the narrow catwalk, he removed the ammunition bandoliers from his shoulders and carefully laid them down within easy reach. He checked his own two pistols and the one he had taken from Butch, stuck one in his waistband and grasped the others. The train could stop at any time now; he was as ready as he ever would be.

In the cab, Butch finished mentally counting off two minutes and said, "Okay. *Now.*"

The engineer eyed the gun pointed at him and said, "You got wet bullets. Wet bullets won't fire."

"You want to test that theory?" Butch said gently.

The engineer hastily reached up and pulled the brake.

Captain Prewitt stood at the end of the coach and surveyed the men of his special detachment with mild irritation. You couldn't plunk troopers down in a railroad coach like this and expect them to maintain full military order, but they seemed excessively relaxed—lounging in the plush seats, playing cards, sleeping, chatting with some of the girls who had drifted in from the passenger car. They *were* on duty, after all. . . .

As he made his way down the aisle, one of the

210

woman passengers spoke to him. "I've never felt so safe travelin' by train . . . havin' all you soldiers on board."

"Well," Prewitt said, "we'll do what we can to see you through safely, ma'am. We—"

He staggered into her as the train lurched to an abrupt stop; troopers and passengers sprawled in the aisle, and the sleepers came awake cursing.

"What're we stoppin' for?" a sleepy private asked.

"Don't see nothin'," said a corporal next to him. He unlatched the coach window he sat by and peered out, then pulled his head back quickly at the boom of a gunshot that seemed to have come from much too near his right ear.

There was a fusillade of shots from the top of the car, and the heavy trampling of feet. A window shattered as a slug came through it, finding its target with a metallic clang in a spittoon in the aisle.

Amid the sudden fury of gunfire, yelling, and shrieks from the women, Prewitt made a rapid estimation of the force attacking them, from the rate of gunfire and the sound of boots on the roof: three at least.

The man in the white straw skimmer was, as usual, a length ahead of his two silent companions, riding swiftly toward the distant S.P. tracks. When the sound of gunfire far-off drifted to them, he stiffened for a moment, then angled his horse toward it and dug in his spurs.

CHAPTER TWENTY-ONE

As the train ground to its sudden stop, Butch leaped down from the cab, holding an iron bucket filled with water, and sprinted past the tender toward the express car. At its door, he stopped and looked toward the rear of the train, grinned and shook his head admiringly. Sundance was blazing away and bouncing all over the roof—the folks in the car would have to think there was an army of desperadoes at work there!

Sundance moved to the other side of the car; a window slid open and a head emerged. Butch snapped off a shot in its general direction—noting that a wet bullet *would* fire, sometimes—and it popped back in as abruptly as a startled turtle.

He turned his attention to the door of the express car, and so missed seeing two cavalrymen slide out of the coach, slip under it, and begin a stealthy crawl toward the engine, with guns drawn.

"Listen in there!" Butch called. "This is a holdup! Open up!"

"You can't rob this train," said a voice from inside. "We got cavalry on board."

"People keep telling me," Butch said. "Now you do what I *say* and open up!" He dashed water from the bucket against the door, as noisily as he could.

"What's that?" the voice from inside wanted to know.

"Kerosene."

"What're ya doin' with kerosene?"

Butch grabbed a stick and raked it along the side of the car in a convincing imitation of a wooden match being struck. "Well, I'm holding a lit match in my hand. Want to take a guess?"

The door slid open with a bang. The express messenger looked quickly at the stick in Butch's hand, and grimaced ruefully. Urged by the gun Butch held on him, he silently began stacking money boxes by the door.

Butch looked toward the rear of the train once more and added a few random shots to the barrage Sundance was keeping up. He gestured toward the boxes. "How much in each of them?"

"Twenty-five thousand," the messenger said.

"We'll take two."

"There's more," the messenger said.

"Thanks," Butch said politely, "but my friend's in kind of a hurry and I can only manage two." He tugged the nearest box out by one handle, then grasped the other, staggering as he took its full weight.

"You want me to give you a hand with the other one?" the messenger asked.

Butch looked up at him. "Why are you being so helpful?"

"This is fun," the messenger said. "You know how boring it gets riding in that express car."

Butch nodded toward the rear. "Right back there."

Panting, he and the messenger ran with the boxes alongside the train. At the gap between the express car and the first coach, Butch jerked his head to the side. The messenger ducked between the two cars, followed by Butch.

"Now up." He nodded toward an iron ladder leading to the top of the express car. The messenger ran his eyes up it, then looked questioningly at Butch.

"You climb up and I'll hand 'em up to you."

The messenger nodded and scrambled up the ladder. Butch peered out from between the cars. One or two passengers had their heads stuck out of the coach windows. Butch sent two shots their way and they disappeared. Straining at the effort, he managed to hoist the money boxes up to where the messenger could reach them and lift them the rest of the way to the roof, then climbed the ladder.

The two soldiers who had been cautiously working their way along under the train reached the express car just in time to look up and see him disappear out of their line of fire. They cursed, turned, and began to crawl back the way they had come.

The conductor came from the forward coach and burst into the scene of confused turmoil in the cavalry car. "They're robbin' the express car!" he yelled to Prewitt.

"I see," Prewitt said calmly. "Is anyone hurt in the other car?"

"No, but aren't you gonna do nothin' to stop 'em?"

"Not yet," Prewitt replied. "If *we* start firing, a lot of civilians could be killed. We'll wait."

"But—"

"Sir! We are the United States Cavalry. When they try to get away, we'll be down on them like a hawk on a chicken!" He glared at the conductor. "Like I said, we'll wait."

The conductor winced at the sound of a fresh flurry of shots from above and the sound of trampling feet on the coach roof.

Sundance, followed by the money-laden messenger and Butch, paused at the rear edge of the coach and checked his pistol. "Let's hope they don't get brave all of a sudden. I've got about five shots left."

He eyed the gap between the coach and the cattle car that housed the cavalry mounts, then leaped it. On the other side, he turned and motioned for Butch to jump. He could hear the snorting and stamping of the agitated horses beneath him.

Butch hefted the money box, and decided it was no

214

case for a standing jump. He retreated ten feet along the catwalk, then ran forward, pushing off with all his might as he reached the gap.

His left foot struck the edge of the cattle car; the impact jarred the box from his grip, but momentum carried it forward to land on the roof. He teetered for a second, then began to topple backward between the cars. Sundance's frantic grab caught one ankle and left him dangling upside down, facing the cavalry coach.

A sergeant in the car saw him through the vestibule door and yelled, "They're comin' in!" He leveled his pistol at Butch, but the milling crowd prevented a clear shot.

The two crawling soldiers peered up as they reached the gap and saw the inverted form suspended above them. "What the hell's that?" one muttered.

"Dunno. No friend of ours, for sure," the other said, and rolled on his back to take aim.

Leaning out from the cab, the engineer and fireman could get only a confused view of the action on the roof, but were aware that they were no longer facing any direct threat. "Let's see if we can shake 'em off," the engineer said. He yanked the brake release and the reverse lever. The train lurched and began to back up down the track.

The supine soldier with his gun trained on Butch gave a cry of panic as it was knocked from his hand by the bottom of the moving coach; he and his companion tried to flatten themselves as the coach's understructure passed over them. Once the rear wheel truck passed them, they rolled out from under and jumped into the open door of the express car as it came by.

The jolt of the train's start-up nearly pitched Sundance from the roof, but he kept his balance and his grip on Butch's ankle, sending a furious and impotent shot to ping off the engine cab. A mighty heave brought Butch up, to sprawl, cursing, on the cattle-car roof.

Two shots from below shattered the glass of the coach's vestibule door but passed harmlessly above their heads. Sundance eyed the door. It opened, and the sergeant stepped out; Sundance drove him back with a slug that struck splinters from the door frame.

Butch, now on his knees, caught his breath and shook his head, then looked across to the coach roof. The messenger was standing holding the second money box, patiently enough, but with a dubious look on his face.

"I'd rather not try that, if you don't mind," he called to them.

"Okay," Butch said. He got to his feet and balanced against the motion of the train. "Throw me the box."

The messenger nodded, drew his arms back, and gave the box a powerful but awkward start on its journey through the air. Butch and Sundance grabbed for it, but the throw was short; it hit the edge of the cattle-car roof and rebounded into the space between the cars.

The pang of rage and regret that Butch and Sundance felt was for an instant shared by the two troopers who had poked their heads outside the coach door in time to be slammed into unconsciousness by the plummeting box, which then struck the roadbed and burst open. In an instant, greenbacks were scattered across the desert, as if some strange form of plant life had suddenly sprung up there.

Butch and Sundance turned away from the melancholy spectacle and opened a hatch on top of the cattle car.

In the express car, the two winded soldiers brightened as they discovered the troop's Gatling gun, broken down for carrying, but easily reassembled. In a moment they had it together, and were hoisting it up the ladder to the roof of the car.

Sundance swung down into the cattle car, landing neatly on one of the horses. He looked through the open hatch and stretched his arms to receive the remaining money box from Butch. "*Jesus*, this damn thing is heavy."

"Try *running* with it," Butch said briefly as he clambered through the hatch and dropped to the floor. With Sundance's help he manhandled the box onto a pack-saddled horse and began lashing its handles to the saddle.

A glance through the slats at the end of the car showed movement: more troopers braving the perils of the coach door. Butch nodded in their direction. "Better discourage them a little."

Sundance took careful aim and fired; then again. The door to the coach closed with an emphatic bang. Sundance squeezed the trigger once more; the hammer clicked on an empty chamber.

The old water-tank tender and his wife sat in rush chairs in front of their shanty and gazed with fascination at the reversing train, which was slowing as it approached them. The two secretive bathers in the water tank would have been excitement enough for one day, but this was a whole week's worth. A month's, maybe.

Butch pushed through the crowd of horses to the sliding door at the side of the car, shoved his hand through the slatting, and felt for the latch. His fingers slid off it; he could not get enough purchase on it to open it. Working with urgent haste, he slipped off his jacket and unbuttoned his suspenders, and gestured fiercely at Sundance to remove his. This done, he tied both pairs together, scrambled onto a horse's back and through the hatch.

On the roof, he held one end of the suspenders and lashed the other to the hatch cover and dropped it over the side. A looming presence at the edge of his vision sent him diving to lie flat on the roof; the spout of the water tank passed inches above his head.

"All barrels loaded," one of the troopers reported as the two of them set the Gatling down on the express car roof. "Now we c'n show those—shit, *duck!*"

They flattened to the catwalk as the spout neatly swept the superweapon from it to crash alongside the roadbed.

"My enlistment's up next year," one said. "I was plannin' to re-up. Don't know as I will."

"Do," the other said. "Then you c'n lend me your bonus money so's I c'n buy out of the rest of *my* stretch."

The heavy hatch cover, bobbing at the end of the improvised elastic, finally hit the door latch and hammered it open just as the train came to a stop. From inside the car Sundance slid the door aside with a mighty shove. Panicked—or at the least highly annoyed—horses began leaping from the car and heading for all points of the horizon at the gallop.

Butch dove through the hatch and onto a horse, just managing to get his foot into a stirrup before the animal pounded to the open door and jumped through it. The jolt of its landing on the hard ground nearly threw him, but he contrived to keep in the saddle and gain control of his mount. He glanced behind him. There came the horse with the money box lashed on, wild-eyed and ready to run; then Sundance, firmly mounted, and letting out an exultant whoop.

Butch rose in his stirrups with an answering yell; and, in the midst of the thundering herd of freed horses, Butch Cassidy and the Sundance Kid rode hell-for-leather for the far place where the sky met the earth.

"All *right*, men!" Prewitt called, once the train had again come to a halt and it was clear that the robbery, attack, insurrection, or whatever the hell the shooting had been about, was over and that the action against the bandits could be joined on some ground well away from inconveniently vulnerable civilians, "let's go get 'em. Mount up!" He clapped his hands smartly together and charged out the door, almost tripping on the coach steps in his zeal.

The sight of the gaping door of the cattle car and its vacant interior, only a few piles of droppings showing that a dozen prime cavalry mounts had ever occupied it, struck him like a blow. He whirled and saw a cloud of dust receding toward the south. And the east. *And* the northwest . . .

The thudding of hoofbeats snapped him to alertness. But it was not any of his strayed charges approaching him, but three lathered, weary animals, bearing riders.

"Are you in charge?" asked the grim-faced, straw-hatted man on the lead horse.

Prewitt gave him a morose look. An honest answer would be that he didn't seem to be in charge of *anything* just now.

"We need fresh horses," the man said.

Prewitt grinned mirthlessly. "Take all you goddam want." His wave included most of the landscape. "They're right out there."

Le Fors glared, took in the significance of the dwindling dust clouds and the empty car, wrenched the straw skimmer from his head and, in a wordless rage, scaled it into the air.

They were in open country now, the horses settled into an easy trot, and heading for high ground.

"I guess we'll be famous, huh?" Sundance asked. He looked back affectionately at the richly laden pack horse he led.

"I'd say you'll get your poster, Sundance," Butch said.

"Sonofa*bitch*," Sundance remarked in wonder after a while. "We're gonna be *famous*."

Butch quirked an eyebrow. This was one time he

wasn't about to give Sundance an argument. They crested a ridge, moving along easily, unhurried. "You did some pretty fancy shooting back there, did I mention that?"

"Just soldiers," Sundance said modestly.

Their eyes and ears were keener than most men's. If anyone could have heard and seen some years ahead and thousands of miles away, to a restaurant patio and the wall beyond it, the wall that would hide a hundred soldiers until they rose to pour death from a hundred rifles, Butch and Sundance could have. If they had, they might, even now in the full flush of their triumph, have ridden other trails . . .

"Give me a bunch of soldiers *any* time," the Sundance Kid said happily, with a broad grin. Butch Cassidy grinned back.

. . . but more likely not.